W9-AMN-101

DEVILS IN DAYLIGHT

ALSO BY TANIZAKI FROM NEW DIRECTIONS

A Cat, a Man, and Two Women

The Maids

DEVILS IN DAYLIGHT

Junichiro Tanizaki

Translated by J. Keith Vincent

A NEW DIRECTIONS BOOK

Translation copyright © 2017 by J. Keith Vincent

All rights reserved. Except for brief passages quoted in a newspaper, magazine, radio, television, or website review, no part of this book may be reproduced in any form or by any means, electronic or mechanical, including photocopying and recording, or by any information storage and retrieval system, without permission in writing from the Publisher.

Published by arrangement with Chuokoron-Shinsha and the Wylie Agency.

Manufactured in the United States of America
New Directions Books are printed on acid-free paper
First published as a New Directions Book in 2017

Library of Congress Cataloging-in-Publication Data
Names: Tanizaki, Jun'ichirō, 1886–1965, author. | Vincent, Keith 1968– translator.
Title: Devils in daylight / Junichiro Tanizaki ; translated by J. Keith Vincent
Other titles: Hakuchū kigo. English
Description: New York : New Directions Publishing Corporation, 2017.
| "A New Directions book."
Identifiers: LCCN 2016037891 | ISBN 9780811224918 (alk. paper)
Subjects: LCSH: Witnesses—Fiction. | Code and cipher stories. | Murder—Fiction.
| GSADF: Mystery fiction. | Suspense fiction.
Classification: LCC PL839.A7 H313 2017 | DDC 895.63/44--dc23
LC record available at https://lccn.loc.gov/2016037891

10 9 8 7 6 5 4 3 2 1

New Directions Books are published for James Laughlin
by New Directions Publishing Corporation
80 Eighth Avenue, New York 10011

DEVILS IN DAYLIGHT

SONOMURA MADE NO SECRET OF THE FACT THAT mental illness ran in his family. I had contracted an intimacy with him nonetheless, and associated with him in full awareness of how impetuous, how aberrant of mind, and how willful he could be. And yet even I could not suppress my astonishment when he telephoned that morning. This time, it seemed, Sonomura really had been stricken with lunacy. It was the same time of year as now; the season, they say, when madness spreads most easily. The suffocating June air, along with the explosion of green on the leaves, must have caused some perturbation in my friend's brain. There was no other way to explain the phone call, I thought. Indeed, I instantly believed this to be the reason. The call came, if memory serves, at around ten in the morning.

"Ahh!! Takahashi, is that you?" he said, jumping in as soon as he heard my voice. He was extremely agitated.

"Listen, I need you to come over here immediately. There is something you have to see."

"I would love nothing more my friend! But today won't do. I'm writing a serial novel for a magazine and I have to finish the manuscript by two o'clock today. I've been up all night writing."

This was not a lie. My pen had not left my hand since the night before and I had not slept a wink. Sonomura was the spoiled son of wealthy parents, just the type to call a person up out of the blue like this, with no regard for their circumstances, and demand their presence for a game of show-and-tell. I felt a ripple of irritation.

"All right then! Get over here as fast as you can, as soon as you finish writing. I'll wait here for you until three."

This only made me angrier.

"I told you today is no good. I got no sleep last night and now I am dead tired. When I finish writing, I plan to head straight for the bath and then get some sleep. Whatever it is that you're so keen to show me can wait until tomorrow, can it not?"

"No, it has to be today. Otherwise it will be too late. And if you won't come with me, I'll have no choice but to go by myself..."

As he said these words, he lowered his voice to a whisper and continued:

"What I am about to tell you is a secret. You are not to breathe a word of it to another soul! Later tonight, at around one o'clock, in a certain part of Tokyo, a crime... a homicide will be performed. I want to get ready now and go see it happen, and I want you to go as well. So what do you say? Will you join me?"

"What? What will be performed?" I asked again, unable to believe my ears.

"A murder... a murder is going to be committed," he said, this time using the English word.

"How do you know this? And who, might I ask, is going to kill whom?"

These words came out much louder than I had intended. Startled by the sound of my own voice, I looked around nervously. Fortunately my wife and children showed no signs of having heard.

"Listen, Takahashi. Please stop screaming into the telephone... I don't know who's going to kill whom. And even if I did, I wouldn't tell you the details over the telephone. What I can tell you is that this very night, at a certain location, a certain person is going to put an end to a certain someone else's life. This is all I have been able to get wind of so far. Of course I am not personally involved with the crime, so I am responsible neither for preventing it, nor for reporting it. But I want to watch it happen, in secret, without any of those involved knowing that I am there. And I would feel a lot better about it if you came with me. Doesn't that sound more enjoyable than staying home writing a novel?"

Sonomura said this with an eerily calm and quiet voice. But the calmer he became, the more I began to question his state of mind. As he spoke I felt my entire body begin to tremble and shudder.

"How can you speak so earnestly about something so outrageous? Have you lost your mind?"

This is what I should have said, but the truth is that I was so afraid for my poor friend's sanity that I did not find the courage to utter these words. I felt a dreadful panic rising inside me.

Sonomura had always used the ample time and money he had at his disposal to pursue an extravagant lifestyle. Recently, however, he had grown tired of ordinary pleasures and had become increasingly obsessed with moving pictures and crime novels. His fantasy life grew more bizarre with each passing day, and now it seemed to have intensified to the point of insanity. The thought made my hair stand on end. He had no real friends besides myself, no parents, no wife, and no children of his own. He spent his days alone with his tens of thousands of yen, and if he really had lost his mind, I was the only person who could look after him. It was clear that if I did not want his nerves to take a turn for the worse, I would have to go and pay him a visit as soon as my work was done.

"All right then. If that's how it is, I'll go to see it with you. Just be sure to wait for me. I think I can finish writing by two and get to your place by three. I might be half an hour, or even an hour late—but I want you to wait until I arrive."

My greatest concern was that he would set out by himself before I got there.

"Are we agreed then? I will be there by four at the latest, so you stay put and wait for me. All right? Can you promise me that?"

After repeatedly confirming his reply, I hung up the receiver at last.

I must confess that while I tried my best to concentrate on the manuscript on my desk until two in the afternoon, my thoughts were in complete disarray, and my attention was hopelessly scattered. All I could do was keep running my pen across the paper, writing god knows what, scratching out just enough nonsense to fulfill my obligation to the magazine.

To pay a sick call to a mad man: as Sonomura's only friend, it was my duty, but it was a far from pleasant one. To begin with, my own state of mental health is hardly sound enough to qualify me to look after someone like him. As you might expect from a close friend of someone like Sonomura, I myself suffer from bouts of neurasthenia. The symptoms come every year around this time when the leaves turn green, and I could see the signs of them coming on this year as well. If I was going to visit this lunatic while in such a delicate state myself, there was no telling when his sickness might pass on to me, and the mummy-hunter, as they say, would end up mummified himself. What's more, even if this murder that Sonomura believed was going to take place that evening did in fact happen—highly unlikely as it was—I had neither the curiosity nor the courage to go with him to see. Were I to witness a murder, I was liable to go mad even before Sonomura. But I take my friendships very seriously, so I had no choice but to bite the bullet and pay him a visit to see just how bad things were.

It was ten after two o'clock by the time I put my manuscript out of its misery. After staying up all night, I am normally dead to the world until evening at least. But I had promised Sonomura to be at his place by four o'clock, and the excitement of the situation kept my fatigue at bay. I fortified myself with a glass of wine, dressed in my navy-blue summer suit for the first time that season, and boarded the train for Mita at the Hakusan-Ue stop. Sonomura's house was close to the grounds of Shiba Park.

As the train jostled me to and fro, my thoughts ran in a new, terrifying direction: What if this story Sonomura had told me on the phone was in fact not a lie at all? Perhaps it was actually possible for him to predict that on that very night, somewhere in the city, someone would be murdered! In order for him to see the murder take place, perhaps it was necessary for me to accompany him to the scene of the crime—in other words, what if he was planning to kill me with his own hands that evening? "I'll show you a murder," he had said—but having lured me to the scene, was he not planning to perpetrate that murder himself, with me as the victim? The idea might seem preposterous, even comical. But it was not completely without merit. Of course, I had no intention of offering myself as a sacrifice in such a cruel game. I had never given Sonomura cause to resent me, and as far as I knew there was no misunderstanding between us. Rationally speaking, he had no reason whatsoever to want me dead. But what if he had lost his mind? In that case, my fear might not be so outlandish. After all, what was to stop a person on a steady diet of the most atrocious crime fiction from getting it into his head to murder a good friend? No, there was nothing the slightest bit unnatural about that; it was well within the realm of possibilities.

As my head filled with these thoughts I came close to getting off the train right then and there. My forehead broke out in a cold sweat and for a moment I felt the blood flowing through my heart come to a stop. Then, in the next instant, a new wave of fear invaded my breast with the force of a tsunami.

Might the very fact that I was letting this absurd notion upset me so much be a sign that I myself was going mad? What if Sonomura's madness had already transmitted itself to me, just now, over the telephone?

This possibility seemed even more plausible than my earlier concerns, and even more frightening. Not wanting to believe that I myself was the lunatic, I struggled to banish these thoughts from my mind.

Clearly, I told myself, I am fretting over sheer nonsense. Didn't Sonomura just tell me that he had nothing to do with the crime himself, and that he had no idea who the perpetrator and who the victim would be? He only said that he'd caught wind that a murder would be performed for some unknown reason. Looked at in this way, it was highly unlikely that he was planning to murder me. His madness has caused him to mistake a flight of fancy for reality, and he wants me to go with him to confirm what he did or did not see. This was the only rational interpretation of the matter, so why on earth did I permit myself to engage in such ludicrous conjectures? The whole situation was absurd.

Mumbling these words to myself I endeavored to scoff at the state of my own nerves, and yet even after I disembarked from the train at Onarimon Station and came as far as Sonomura's house, I had not fully made up my mind to go through with the meeting. I walked straight past the side of his house and paced back and forth two or three times between the Sangedatsu-mon and the Daimon Gates of Zōjōji Temple. After much hesitation and ambling about in this fashion, I finally turned back to Sonomura's house, having resigned myself to whatever might be in store for me.

Upon opening the ornately decorated door to his impressive study, I found Sonomura walking around the European-style room, casting nervous glances at a clock resting on the mantelpiece. I noted with satisfaction that the time was four o'clock exactly. Sonomura had a slender build and cut a dashing figure in Western-style clothes. He was dressed and ready to go out, sporting an elegant black jacket and trousers with understated vertical stripes, a white satin tie with green embroidery, and a tie pin set with alexandrite—the man had a weakness for precious stones. Pearl and aquamarine rings glittered on his delicate, slightly trembling fingers, and a nugget of turquoise hung from a gold chain in the center of his chest, like the compound eye of an insect.

"Why, it's four o'clock on the dot! Awfully decent of you to come, my good man!"

As Sonomura turned his face toward me to say this, I paid special attention to his pupils. They had their usual unnatural luster, but I detected no added fierceness or frenzy. With some relief I took a seat in an easy chair in a corner of the room.

"So tell me. This story of yours, is it really true?" I said, making an obvious effort to relax, savoring a long drag from my cigarette.

"Yes it is. I have certain proof."

Although he continued to pace nervously, he pronounced these words with complete conviction.

"Listen, Sonomura. Enough of this infernal pacing back and forth. Please have a seat and tell me the whole story. You said the crime was going to take place late tonight, did you not? If that is the case, we still have ample time."

I thought it best to begin by treading gently and helping him calm his nerves.

"I have proof that it will happen, as I said, but I have yet to establish where. I must find the exact location before it grows too dark. I don't expect we'll be in any danger, but I do hope you are willing to accompany me."

"Absolutely. I came here intending to go with you, and that is still my plan. But tell me, what hope do you have of finding the place without at least some clue as to where it is?"

"Oh, but I do have quite a good educated guess. By my calculations, the crime will take place in Mukōjima!" Overjoyed by his own discovery, he answered with such alacrity that the brooding, bad-tempered man I knew seemed momentarily to disappear. Meanwhile, he paced faster and faster.

"How do you know it's in Mukōjima?"

"I shall explain it all to you afterward. Right now we have to make haste. It is not every day you have a chance to watch a murder happen, and it would be a terrible shame to miss it."

"But if you do know the location after all, what need is there to rush? It is only half an hour by taxi to Mukōjima and the sun sets late these days so we have a good two or three hours before it gets dark. Why not fill me in a little more before we go? If you drag me off on this wild-goose chase now without telling me all the details, you will be having a fine time of it, but where's the fun for me?"

This reasoning seeming to have penetrated even Sonomura's overheated brain, he nodded repeatedly, blowing little snorts of air out of his nostrils.

"Oh, all right! I shall bring you up to speed then," he said, keeping an eye on the clock and reluctantly taking a seat in a chair opposite me. He felt around in a pocket in the back of his jacket for a crumpled piece of lined paper, and spread it out on the marble-topped tea table between us.

"This slip of paper is the proof I mentioned. It came into my possession in an odd place two nights ago. You will no doubt recognize the letters written here." He said this in a grandiloquent tone, as if posing a riddle, while looking straight at me with a slightly queer smile and upturned eyes.

On the paper someone had written in pencil a mixture of symbols and numbers that might have been a mathematical formula of some kind: 6*;48*634;‡1;48† 85;4‡12?††45 ... It went on like this for two or three lines. Of course I had no idea what any of it meant. And if I was already more than a little worried about Sonomura's state of mind, now that he had produced this paper as proof of some dastardly crime, what little doubt I might have entertained of my poor friend's insanity was put finally to rest.

"So what, pray tell, is this? I can't make heads or tails of these symbols. You no doubt plan to enlighten me as to their meaning?"

As I said these words I was conscious that my face had gone pale and my voice was trembling.

"For a literary man, you're not very well read, are you?"

He suddenly doubled over and cackled with laughter, whereupon he continued, with immense self-satisfaction, like some insufferable scholar showing off his vast learning.

"I take it you have not read Poe's famous story 'The Gold Bug.' Anyone who had read it would recognize these symbols immediately."

Sadly, I had only read two or three of Poe's stories. I had heard of one with the title "The Gold Bug," but I had no idea what it was about.

"If you do not know Poe's tale, it is no surprise that you can't read these symbols. Allow me to give you a brief summary ... A long time ago there was a pirate named Captain Kidd who buried a treasure somewhere in South Carolina, and used a secret cipher, or 'cryptograph,' to record its location. Subsequently, one William Legrand of Sullivan's Island, South Carolina, happening upon this record, managed to decode the cryptograph, locate the treasure, and excavate it. This is more or less what happens in the story. But the interesting part is where Legrand explains how he cracked the cryptographic code, which he does in great detail. This slip of paper that came into my possession two days ago contains a clear example of Captain Kidd's cipher. So when I found it lying about where someone had left it, I knew immediately that some scheme or crime was afoot, and made sure to pick it up."

Not having read Poe's story myself, I had no way of knowing how much of Sonomura's account was accurate. So unfortunately, at least for the time being, I had no choice but to bow to his superior knowledge.

"Mmm. Hmm … Now things are getting interesting. So tell me, where precisely did you pick up this scrap of paper?"

Like a mother listening raptly to her child tell a story, I encouraged Sonomura to go on with his, but inside I was thinking to myself that there are few things more insufferable than an overeducated lunatic trying to impress an ignoramus. I sat back and listened, wondering what sort of balderdash he would come out with next.

"This is how I came into possession of this piece of paper … Picture me, at around seven o'clock the night before last, alone, as always, seated in the first-class section of the Park Club Theater in Asakusa, watching a moving picture. As I think you know, the first two or three rows of seats at that particular theater are reserved for couples, and the remainder are for men only. It was a Saturday night, and both floors of the place were packed when I came in. But before long I spotted an open seat in the front row of the men's section. Which is to say that I was sitting right on the border between the men's and the mixed sections, and the seats in front of me were filled with couples. At first I paid the latter no attention, but before long I realized that something quite extraordinary was taking place right under my nose, causing me to forget all about the picture and to find my attention riveted instead by these other goings on. At some point a group consisting of two men and a woman had taken the seats directly in front of me. It was so crowded one could barely breathe and people were standing even in the first-class section, creating a wall of people, and making my surroundings even darker than usual …

"For that reason I couldn't really make out the clothing or the faces of these three individuals in front of me. All I could tell from behind was that one of them was a woman with a pompadour hairdo and the other two were men. From the sheer volume and sultry weight of the woman's hair, I guessed that she was relatively young. One of the men had his hair in a severe, glossy part, and the other had a crewcut. The woman in the pompadour was furthest to the right, the man with parted hair in the middle, and the man with the crewcut was on the left. This seating order clearly indicated that the woman was either the wife or the mistress of the man in the middle—at any rate someone in an intimate relation to him, while the man on the left was perhaps a friend of the man in the middle.... You will no doubt agree with my construal of the situation. If the woman were in the same kind of a relationship with both men, she would have sat between them, but if she were closer to one than the other, the one she was closer to would be sure to insert himself between her and the other man.... You would assume the same, would you not Takahashi?"

"Yes, I suppose I would. But why the concern with this woman's relationship?"

And why, I wondered, did he have to explain something so obvious as if he were a master detective explicating some brilliant feat of ratiocination?

"That relationship, my friend, is the crux of this story. You remember those strange happenings that I mentioned earlier? Well this woman and the man with the crewcut on the left were each reaching one arm behind their seats, holding hands and exchanging queer signals to each other, all without the man in the middle's knowledge. The woman would trace some letters with her fingertips on the man's palm, and then the man would do the same in reply. The two of them carried on like this for quite some time."

"Sounds to me like they were making plans for a secret rendezvous without the other man knowing. This kind of thing happens all the time. What, pray tell, is so strange about that?"

"I wanted to know what they were writing, so I watched the movements of their fingers ..."

Sonomura had completely ignored my attempt to throw cold water on his story; he continued as if in a soliloquy, now with even more intensity.

"They were tracing simple characters with their fingers. I easily determined that they were characters from the *katakana* alphabet. Luckily, since I was sitting directly behind the man in the middle, and the other two were positioned on either side, the whole thing was playing out right in front of me. No sooner had I understood they were using *katakana* than the woman began to move her finger over the man's palm again. My eyes locked with fierce concentration on her fingertips, and I saw that she was writing the words 'drugs no rope better.' The man was having trouble understanding this, so she patiently rewrote it a number of times. When he finally did understand, he replied with 'when good?' And the woman wrote, 'in 2, 3 days' ... It was at this moment that the man in the middle shifted his body slightly, causing the two quickly to withdraw their hands and to display a look of total absorption in what was happening on screen. Unfortunately, this was the end of their secret communication. But what could 'drugs no rope better' mean? The other phrases, 'when good?' and 'in 2, 3 days' could easily refer to a secret assignation. But the mention of drugs and rope clearly meant that the woman was plotting to do something horrific to the man in the middle, and to do it *with a rope rather than poison.*"

Now to anyone who was ignorant of the state of Sonomura's mental health at the time, this account might well seem perfectly rational and persuasive. Even I was tempted to be drawn in by it at first. But as I thought about it more carefully I realized how implausible it was. Yes, it was dark in the theater—but what sort of fool plans a murder via *katakana* syllables in the presence of so many people? Surely Sonomura, under the spell of some sort of hallucination, had simply misread the messages the man and woman were exchanging in such a manner that fueled his fantasy. At first I was inclined to disabuse him of this fantasy, which I could easily have done with a few well-chosen words. But being curious as to how far his madness would go, I kept my mouth shut and continued to observe him instead.

"Having realized the nature of their plans, I found myself more intrigued than horrified, and desperately wanting to know more of their secret communications. When and where would this crime be committed? I began to itch with curiosity, and felt an uncontrollable desire to be there when it happened, so as to watch it in secret. Fortunately, at just that moment, the two extended their hands again, ever so slowly, behind their chairs. This time the woman's hand held what I took to be a crumpled slip of paper, which she transferred to the man's hand, whereupon they both withdrew their arms again. As I devoured this scene with my eyes, you may imagine how desperately I wanted to know what was written on that slip of paper … No sooner had the man taken hold of it than he stood up to go to the bathroom, presumably to read it, and returned five minutes later. He then coughed into his hands and discarded the paper nonchalantly, as if it were a used tissue, behind his seat. It landed right at my feet and I quietly covered it with my shoe."

"What a reckless fellow!" I said, in a half-joking tone. "Why not discard the paper while he was in the bathroom?"

"I had the same thought myself. But perhaps he forgot to throw it out while he was in the bathroom and simply got rid of it hastily as soon as he realized he was still holding it? Since the message was written using the cryptograph, he no doubt thought he could throw it out anywhere without cause for worry. Certainly he never imagined that someone capable of reading the cipher was sitting directly behind him!"

As Sonomura said this, he laughed delightedly.

Just then the clock struck five, but luckily Sonomura was so caught up in his tale that he failed to notice.

"I planned to get a good look at the three of them after the picture ended and the lights came up in the theater, but they did not stick around too long. Just as the man with the crewcut discarded the paper, the woman let out a sigh of apparent boredom and set about convincing the man in the middle that it was time to leave. Her voice was sugary and willful, like that of child begging for a sweet. Presently the man with the crewcut chimed in as well, agreeing that the film was a bore and also urging the other man to leave. Thus pressed on both sides, the man in the middle reluctantly rose to his feet, and the three of them finally quit the theater. Judging from the whole context, it was clear to me that the woman and the man with the crewcut had no interest in the movie to begin with, and had only come there to take advantage of the crowded darkness in order to carry out their clandestine communication. After they had left, it was a simple enough matter for me to retrieve the slip of paper from the floor."

"What, then, do the cryptograms on this slip of paper signify? Please explain—I am all ears!"

"As anyone who has read Poe's story would know, the numbers and symbols here all represent letters of the alphabet. The number

'5,' for example, stands for the letter 'a,' '2' for 'b,' and '3' for 'g.' The symbol '†' represents the letter 'd,' '*' stands for 'n,' ';' for 't,' and '?' for 'u.' If you convert the cryptograms into the letters of the alphabet they represent, adding punctuation where appropriate, you get this strange English sentence:

> In the night of the Death of the Buddha, at the time of the Death of Diana, there is a scale in the north of Neptune, where it must be committed by our hands.

"Are you following me? This is the sentence it becomes, except for the fact that the cipher for the letter 'w' does not appear in Poe's story, so the author has substituted the symbol for 'v.' As for the capitals 'D,' 'B,' and 'N,' there is no special cipher in the code for these, but I took the liberty of adding them in order to make it easier for you to read."

After translating the English sentence into Japanese for my benefit as well, Sonomura continued, "It seems quite impenetrable at first, but if you think about it carefully the meaning becomes clear. 'In the night of the Death of the Buddha' must refer to the *butsumetsu*, the unlucky day that comes four or five days a month according to the old calendar. If you take into account what the woman said at the theater about 'in 2, 3 days,' the *butsumetsu* in question can only be the one that happens to fall today, on this very day. As for, 'at the time of the Death of Diana,' Diana is the goddess of the moon, so this must mean the time when the moon sets. Tonight's moonset will come at 1:36 a.m., so this is when they will commit their crime. Now the phrase 'there is a scale in the north of Neptune' poses more of a challenge. Clearly it refers to the location of the venue they have chosen for the murder, so we have no hope of witnessing it without decoding the meaning of this phrase.

"The word 'Neptune' could of course be a special code word that only the man with the crewcut and the woman with the pompadour know. But then again, since we find it in the company of words like 'Diana,' and 'Buddha,' it may not be that difficult to solve after all. Neptune may refer to the god of the sea or to the planet Neptune, which is of course named after the god. So it must be a place having to do with the sea, or with water. As I was thinking along these lines the first thing that entered my head was the Suijin Shrine in Mukōjima, which, as the name indicates, is dedicated to the god of the sea. As you know, the area around that shrine is extremely desolate and thus highly suitable for the commission of a crime like this. 'There is a scale in the north of Neptune,' suggests that there must be, somewhere to the north of the Suijin Shrine, or the Yaomatsu building next to it, a house or other location bearing a triangular, fish-scale mark. The phrase 'A scale in the north of Neptune' doesn't provide a great deal of information, but this fact in itself must indicate that the mark is located in a place that's relatively easily spotted. As for 'where it must be committed'—the pronoun 'it' can refer to nothing other than the act of murder, as indeed the English verb 'commit' implies a crime. And 'by our hands,' indicates that the woman and the man with the crewcut will be accomplices. If we consider this alongside the phrase 'drugs no rope better,' the riddle unravels fully, and there is no longer any room for doubt. It's a shame that there is no mention of the victim of the crime here, but I think it is safe to assume that they are targeting the man with the shiny part in his hair who sat between them. Of course the identity of the victim is not really our concern in any case. It is more than enough for us to crack the cipher, to establish the time and place of the murder, and to watch from the shadows as it is carried out. We have now only to proceed to Mukōjima and locate the mark of the fish scale…. Now that you have heard my explanation, you see what an unprecedented and intriguing crime this promises to be. I hope you also understand that time is of the essence. I have now wasted a precious hour and a half in reporting all of this to you."

He was right. The clock did indeed read 5:30 p.m., but the lingering sun of early June showed no sign of disappearing any time soon, and the light coming in from the window of his European-style home was still as bright as midday.

"Well, it may have been a waste of time for you, but it was well worth it for me to hear such a riveting story. But tell me, why did you not go looking for the fish-scale mark in the time you had between your visit to the theater and today?"

I was full of advice for my friend, but internally I was at a loss for what to do with him. The fatigue from not having slept the night before had now caught up with me, and had it been possible, I would most willingly have refused to accompany him all the way to Mukōjima. It seemed absurd to play along in his vain attempts at sleuthing. And yet I knew I could never rest if I allowed him to go alone.

"Well I most certainly did not need you to suggest it! I spent the whole day yesterday scouring every corner of the vicinity of the Suijin shrine, but I found no sign of the fish-scale mark. Obviously, the woman was waiting until the day of the murder to inscribe it. No doubt she had gone out and placed the mark somewhere this morning. I did manage to identify a few likely spots during my searches yesterday, so I do not anticipate that it will be too difficult for us to find it today. That said, we can do nothing once it gets dark, so we had best get going as soon as possible. Stand up, my friend. Let us make haste. And take this with you just in case."

Saying this, he took a pistol out of his desk drawer and handed it to me.

He spoke with such passion, and had become so worked up about the whole affair that I knew there was no point in trying to stop him. The best way to make him snap out of it was to accompany him to Mukōjima and let him see for himself that even today there was no such fish-scale mark anywhere to be found. After that, no matter how touched in the head he was, he would have no choice but to acknowledge that he had been imagining the whole thing. Realizing this, I dutifully took the pistol he was offering me, rose to my feet, and said cheerfully, "Off we go then! I shall play Watson to your Sherlock Holmes!"

We hailed a taxi outside of Onarimon Station, and as we sped toward Mukōjima, Sonomura remained preoccupied with his imaginings. He had pulled his soft hat low over his eyes and folded his arms—he appeared to be deep in thought. But the next instant he suddenly perked up and said, "We'll know for certain soon enough, I suppose. But what sort of people, what class of people do you think they are? If only I could have identified the kind of clothing they were wearing the other night. But it was simply too dark to tell. One thing we can say, because they are using the cryptograph from a story by Poe, is that they are not uneducated. In fact they must be quite well read. Don't you agree?"

"Well, yes, I suppose so. I suppose they could be quite high-society for all we know."

"Yes, they could. But then again, perhaps they are not so high-society after all. They could just as easily be part of a major criminal operation, the kind of crooks who think nothing of committing robbery and murder. This would help explain why they used Captain Kidd's cryptograph. It's not an easy code to learn. For an amateur like me the only way to read it is by referring back to Poe's original story and looking up each cipher. And yet the man with the crewcut took only five or six minutes in the bathroom to read the woman's message. This would suggest that they use the code on a regular basis, so much so that they are able to read it as easily if it were written in the regular alphabet. And if that is the case, this would further suggest that they have committed all manner of atrocities for which it was necessary to avail themselves of this cryptographic code. I wager they are no ordinary scoundrels."

Our taxi had passed by the front of Hibiya Park and was now traveling at a great speed along the moat outside the Babasaki Gate of the Imperial Palace.

"Of course, the very fact that we don't know who they are only makes things more intriguing for us," Sonomura continued. "At first I assumed that the motive of their crime had something to do with a love affair. But if they turn out to be serial murderers, there may be other motives in play as well. In any case, we can be sure that tonight at 1:36 a.m., somewhere to the north of the Suijin Shrine, someone is going to be strangled to death with a rope. This is more than enough to keep things interesting, wouldn't you say?..."

By this point the taxi had left the Marunouchi area behind and was heading straight toward Asakusa-bashi.

THREE HOURS LATER, AT AROUND EIGHT IN THE evening, I loaded Sonomora, his slack head lolling about, into a taxi headed back to his place in Shiba.

"So now we know this whole thing was in your head. You seem awfully tense lately. I suggest you focus on calming your nerves. A change of scenery tomorrow would do you a world of good."

As we rocked back and forth in the car, I delivered this lecture to Sonomura, who was sullen and lost in his own thoughts.

From six to eight that evening I had followed Sonomura as he searched all over the vicinity of Suijin, but just as I had suspected, we found no trace of the fish-scale mark. He made a great show of refusing to return home before we found it, but after much pleading and haranguing, I finally convinced him to abandon the search.

"There is something wrong with me recently. Hearing your words just now, I have the feeling I must be going mad . . ."

This he said in a low, groaning voice.

"And yet, it's so strange. The mark must've been there somewhere. . . . My nerves may be frazzled, but there is no mistaking what I saw two nights ago. The mistake must have been mine— something with my interpretation of the letters in the cipher, or my reading of the cryptograph itself. I must go back home and think it all through again."

As he spoke, I found myself both angered and amused by his inability to jettison his crazed imaginings.

"I suppose it can't hurt to think it through once more, but what's the point in taxing your brain so much over something like this? Even if your guess is right, why put yourself through so much trouble to prove it? Listen, I haven't slept since yesterday and I am completely worn out, so I'm going to say goodbye to you for now and head back to my place. I suggest you pack it up too and make it an early night. I'll drop by tomorrow morning to check in on you. Just be sure not to go out by yourself tonight."

He would've had me stay with him all night if I'd let him, so I got out of the taxi at Asakusa-bashi and boarded a train for Kudan. I felt as if I had been bewitched by a fox, and for a while, as I came out of this trance, I felt vaguely disappointed. For those three hours while Sonomura searched the area around Mukōjima, he had not let me stop to eat, and now, suddenly I felt a ravenous hunger. But presently I forgot the hunger as well, thanks to an even stronger wave of fatigue that hit just as I changed from a Jimbo-chō bound train to one headed for Sugamo. Arriving home in Koishikawa, I had the futon put out immediately and fell asleep like a dead man.

I have no idea how many hours I slept, but at some point, still half-dreaming, I heard the asthmatic horn of an automobile and then the sound of someone knocking at the front gate of my house.

My wife called out and woke me, "Darling, there is someone knocking out front! Who could it be at this hour? It sounds like they came here by car."

"He's back! It must be Sonomura! I'm afraid the good doctor has not been himself lately, my dear. But ... Ack!! What a confounded nuisance!"

I had no choice but to rouse myself; I resignedly rubbed my tired eyes, and made my way to the front gate.

"Takahashi! I figured it out! I know where it is now, Takahashi! When they wrote 'Neptune' they didn't mean 'Suijin.' They meant another reference to the god of the sea—the Suitengū Shrine! I had it wrong before! But now I have found the fish-scale mark at last, in a new street just to the north of there!"

I'd opened the side door onto the parterre entryway by the tiniest crack, and when Sonomura lurched through it, he brought his mouth directly to my ear, and vouchsafed this in a conspiratorial whisper.

"We've got to get going! It is now 12:50, so we have only forty-six minutes. I thought of going by myself, but I promised I would take you with me, so I came here first. Hurry up and get ready. We haven't a moment to lose!"

"So you tracked it down at last, did you? But if it's already 12:50 now, I doubt we can make it there in time to catch them at it. And they might even catch us if we aren't careful. I say we should call it a night."

"I won't quit now. Even if I can't see anything, I can at least crouch in the doorway and hear his screams as they choke him to death. The building where the fish-scale mark is, the one I just found, has only one story, with room for a couple of tatami mats inside, so it's got to be very cramped in there. They've taken the paper doors out for the summer and left a couple of reed screens and bamboo blinds. And listen to this: in the back there's a big sitting window and the shutters are full of peepholes and gaps that provide a clear view of the inside. It couldn't be more convenient! Just sitting here and talking we've already lost another ten minutes! It's 1:00 a.m. now. Make up your mind if you're coming or not. If you won't come, I'll go alone."

Who on earth would choose such a spot to commit a murder, I thought. And yet there was no telling what might happen if I let him go alone. The whole affair was a colossal bother, but I had no choice but to go with him.

"All right then. Just a second! Give me a moment to get ready and I'll go with you."

Saying this, I went back inside and quickly changed clothes.

"What is going on, Darling? Where on earth are you going at this hour?" my wife asked, her eyes round with surprise.

"I've been meaning to tell you. Something is up with Sonomura recently. He's been talking nonsense for days. And now he says he wants to go to Suitengū in Ningyōchō because he's convinced that a murder is about to take place there and he wants to watch it happen."

"Oh my word! How dreadful!"

"What really gets me is that he has the nerve to come banging on our door at this hour. But there's no telling what he'll get up to if I leave him to his own devices, so I'll figure out some way to trick him into letting me take him home to Shiba. What a confounded nuisance!"

Leaving my wife with this excuse, I soon found myself once again in the back of a taxi with Sonomura.

The city at midnight was quiet. The car sped straight from Hakusan-Ue past the First Higher School, and from there along the stone-paved train tracks of Hongō Avenue. I still felt like I was dreaming. The early summer sky just before the rainy season was half-obscured by dull rain clouds and scattered with sleepily blinking stars.

"Seventeen minutes! We have only seventeen minutes before it's too late!" said Sonomura, shining a pocket flashlight on the face of his watch as we passed Matsuzumi-chō.

"Only twelve minutes!"

As he said this, the car, as if mimicking Sonomura's crazed manner, took a sudden turn at the corner of Izumibashi onto Ningyō-chō Street.

We got out of the car intentionally at Hettsu-higashi and wound our way through a series of smaller streets in order to avoid passing in front of the police box. I don't know that area well, and since I was simply following Sonomura as he scurried from one dark alleyway into another I couldn't tell exactly where we were. Soon we arrived at the end of a blind alley with two long, squalid-looking houses on either side and wooden slats over an open sewer. Sonomura, who had been hurrying along silently until then, whispered loudly in my ear.

"We're almost there! Step quietly! It's just a few doors down from here!"

"Which one is it? Where is the fish-scale mark?" I asked.

Sonomura did not reply, but stood silently staring at his watch, and then, in a hoarse voice, exclaimed, "Damn it all!"

"Goddamn it! I can't believe it! We are two minutes late. It's thirty-eight minutes past!"

"Yes, but what about the mark? Show me where it is!"

He had spoken with such crazed concentration that I felt the damned fish-scale mark had to be there somewhere, so I kept asking.

"Oh, forget about that blasted mark! I'll explain later! Stop standing there and get over here! Here, I said! Here!"

He grabbed frantically at my shoulder and pulled me into a tight space between two buildings. The eaves on either side came together to shut out the light and there was barely enough room to walk. A strong odor of various rotting things assailed my nostrils in the dark; no doubt from open garbage containers. I felt spiderwebs breaking gently across my earlobes. Sonomura was five or six paces ahead of me and at a certain point he stopped, stifled his breathing, and brought his face directly to a knothole in a storm shutter on the left.

To the right side of the eaves was a solid wall of horizontal siding. But on the left, where Sonomura was currently pressing his face, there was, just as he had said, a large sitting window inset with storm shutters and full of knotholes and gaps through which light came flickering out from the inside. The light was quite strong, giving the impression that the interior of the house was illuminated by an extremely bright electric lamp. I walked right up to it and, standing shoulder to shoulder with Sonomura, put my eye up against another knothole.

The hole was just about wide enough for a thumb to pass through. My eyes had been accustomed to the dark outside, so the bright light inside the room blurred my vision at first, and all I could make out were a few vague shadows. I had a very clear sense, by contrast, of Sonomura's heavy breathing as he stood next to me. In the dead silence of the night, the tick-tock of his wristwatch seemed like the agitated beating of a heart.

After a couple minutes, my vision began to recover. The first thing I saw was an astonishingly white column-like object, lithe as could be, standing bolt upright. I recall that it took me several seconds more before I grasped that this was a long line of flesh just below the beautiful nape of the neck of a woman standing there with her back to me. In fact the woman was positioned so closely to the window that her body threatened to occlude the knothole, making it difficult to recognize as the back of a human being. All I could make out was a squashed Shimada hairdo and a light summer *haori* of black silk gauze that covered her back. The rest, from her waist below, was outside the range of my vision.

The room was by no means large, but for some reason it was lit by an extremely powerful electric light. It was no wonder that I had mistaken the woman's neck for a white column. She was facing slightly downward and the expanse of skin from the nape of her neck to the edge of her clothing was covered in a thick layer of makeup that shone like white lacquer in the blinding light. She was near enough that my nostrils were flooded with the sweet and soft fragrance of her perfume. I felt that I could count each individual strand of her hair. It glistened and gleamed as if she had just stepped out of the hairdresser's; the two side-buns puffed up like the breast feathers of a bird, and the smart chignon with not a single hair out of place, almost like a wig, in shiny black, had a chic and irresistible charm. It was a shame not to be able to see her face, but the gentle, feminine curves of her sloping shoulders, the delicate hairline peeking out of her clothing like the head of a doll, and the alluring musculature between the lobe of her ear and her back was more than enough evidence that this was a woman of astonishing beauty. It was all worth it, I thought, the effort to find this knothole, now that a peek through it had revealed such a woman in such an unexpected place.

It is necessary for me to record a few more of my impressions of the instant when I first saw her, and of the scene I observed over the subsequent minute or two. Even if Sonomura had been mistaken in his predictions, the very fact that such a woman was standing stock still in this way, at this hour, and in a place like this was nothing short of bizarre. The squashed Shimada was evidence that she was no amateur; she was clearly either a geisha or something similar. The elaborate and elegant hair and clothing were those of a woman who followed the latest fashions of the demimonde. And this was no ordinary geisha, but one of the very highest class, perhaps from one of the houses in Shimbashi or Akasaka. But what such a woman was doing in a place like this was more than I could fathom. When I wrote earlier that she was standing "stock still," I meant it quite literally. She was as motionless as a figure in a *tableau vivant*. It was as if she had frozen the exact moment I peeked through the knothole, face turned downward and neck outstretched, as quiet as a fossil—perhaps she had heard our footsteps outside and was listening for more with bated breath?—as this thought occurred to me I hurriedly averted my eyes and looked over at Sonomura, who remained with his face pressed greedily against his own knothole.

Just then someone began moving around inside the house, which had been so hushed until then, and I heard a slight creaking sound, that of someone walking across tatami mats supported by wobbly floor joists. However contemptuous I may have been of Sonomura's madnesss, at some point my own curiosity had gotten the better of me. No sooner did I hear the sound than I was drawn back unthinkingly to the scene inside. I brought my eye to the knothole again.

It had only been a moment—no more than one or two seconds—but the woman had changed her posture and shifted her location. This must have been the cause of the noise I had just heard. Whereas before she had stood directly in front of the knothole so as to block my view, now she had advanced diagonally—the distance of one tatami mat—into the center of the room, thus widening my field of vision considerably so that I could now see almost every corner of the room. Straight ahead, directly opposite the window where I was standing, was a yellowish wall with a peeling wallpaper that one finds in a typical longhouse. To the left was a bamboo screen, and to the right, reed blinds and an exterior veranda closed off with a sliding storm shutter. I had noticed some kind of white object fluttering about near her head, and now I saw it was a man wearing a white cotton *yukata*. He stood pressed up against the wall on her left, facing my direction. He looked to be about eighteen or nineteen, no older than twenty. His hair was cut square in a crewcut, and he was tall, with a swarthy complexion that made him look like a younger version of the last Kikugorō.* The comparison comes to mind not only because he had the crisp good looks of an old-fashioned Edo dandy, but because somewhere, in his cool, narrow eyes and slightly protruding lower lips, there was hint of cunning and coarse slyness that called to mind characters from old kabuki plays like the *Hairdresser Shinza* or the *Rat Boy Thief.***

The expression on the man's face was vivid but impossible to decipher. It was hard to say if he was angry or laughing, calm and careless, or intently concentrating on something. But even more mysterious than this man was a black object that stood in the corner two feet to his left, which looked like some kind of scarecrow. I spent some time contorting my body in different directions in order to position my eyeball in such a way as to discern the true nature of the scarecrow.

Looking more and more closely at it, I saw that the head of the scarecrow was covered in a black velvet cloth, and that it actually stood on three legs ... It was a photographer's camera! That the cramped room was flooded with light, and that the woman had stood so still must've indicated that the man was in the process of taking her photograph. But what could have possibly made it necessary for them to be taking photographs in such a seedy room at this late hour? Did they need, for some reason, to take the photograph in secret?

Naturally I first assumed the man was the producer of some kind of horrific contraband and that he was in the midst of using this woman to manufacture it—this was my first interpretation of the scene.

---

* Onoe Kikugorō V (1844–1903). Kabuki actor known for his realistic acting techniques and for performing in the first motion picture filmed in Japan, in 1889.

** The conniving *Hairdresser Shinza* and the *Rat Boy Thief,* based on the real-life robber of samurai mansions Nakamura Jirokichi (1797–1831), were two roles for which Kikugorō V was well known.

"This is absurd. Some place that damned Sonomura has dragged me to! He must have cottoned on to it himself by now!"

I felt like clapping him on the shoulder and saying, "This is some murder we're about to witness!" Now that I knew the truth of the situation, it was clear that his prediction had been completely off the mark. But then I felt my curiosity surging uncontrollably in a new direction. There was something ludicrous about ending up in front of a scene like this after being taken on a wild ride all around Tokyo yesterday afternoon like the sidekick of some master detective, and yet this was not a laughing matter. It may not have been a murder, but some lesser crime was surely being committed. To be standing here in the dark of night peering through holes in the window shutters just as the scene was playing itself out before my eyes inspired an indescribable terror not unlike that of witnessing a tragic murder, and more than enough to give me a taste of intense anticipation. It was not a sense of normal propriety, then, but the sheer force of shuddering tremors that beset my entire body, that caused me, just barely, to avert my eyes.

And yet the camera continued to stand there on its own and the man showed no sign of lowering his hands. He continued to lean against the wall opposite and stare meaningfully in the woman's direction. And as I watched, for this brief moment he remained as motionless as the woman, those perverse and crafty eyes of his glittering like those of a life-sized carnival doll. The woman still had her back to me, but now she was sitting down on her side, and I could clearly see her figure below the hips. From where the hem of her *haori* lay spread out on the tatami, a spotless white *tabi*-covered foot peeked out halfway, and a long sleeve draped languidly over it. I had only barely caught a glimpse of her upper body before, but now that I could see all of her I confirmed that she was indeed just as voluptuous as I had guessed. What a seductive and supple figure it was! She sat there demurely, without causing a single wrinkle in the thin garment she wore, but that seductive and supple quality somehow suffused every curve of her body with smooth ripples, like a coiling snake. The more I looked—with my eyes widened in surprise and my heart filled with strains of exquisite music—the more I felt flooded with ecstasy.

I was so transfixed by the sight of this beautiful woman that until then I had failed to notice the enormous metal tub that sat on the right side of the room. The presence of such an object in the room was in fact even more mysterious than that of the camera, and I would surely have noticed it long before if the woman had not been there to distract me. It was the size of a Western-style bathtub, an oblong container, narrow but deep, covered in enamel, and it sat there, hulkingly, next to the veranda and the reed blinds.

What were they planning to use this tub for? It certainly was not for bathing, not in a place like this. The camera was on one side, the tub on the other, with the woman sitting in the middle. What could it all mean? ... As I thought about it this way, the purpose of the tub gradually became clear to me. Were they not about to take a photograph that could be titled "Bathing Beauty" or some such? It was a little strange that the woman was wearing a kimono, but perhaps they were just about to start preparing? Perhaps they had been so still because they were planning the angle of the shot. Yes, that must be it! Deciding that this was the case was the only way to solve the mystery of the scene before me ...

As I stood there agreeing with my own conclusion, I kept watch over the two of them inside. But they made no move to prepare. The woman just kept lying there with her eyes cast downward. The man stood still as a pole and continued to glare at the woman's figure. The room was so quiet you could hear a pin drop, and the only moving objects in sight were the man's two eyeballs: they were ogling the area between the woman's chest and her waist, and seemed completely uninterested in anything else. The look in his eyes was too strangely intense for someone who is simply deciding on the angle of a photograph. I traced the line of the man's baleful gaze in order to be certain of where exactly he was concentrating his attention.

There was no doubt about it. No matter how you looked at it, the man's gaze was hovering on the woman's body, between her chest and lap. And not only that, the woman herself, who was also looking down, seemed to be staring at the same area on her own body. From what I could see at my angle, she extended her elbows outward and brought her hands together over her waist, as if she were sewing; she was in the process of fiddling with some kind of object that was resting there. Once I had noticed this, I began to discern the vague outlines of a black lump-like object on her lap. It was *stock still* and seemed to extend quite a ways forward in the shadow of her body.

"Could this be someone—a man—making a pillow of her lap?"

Just as this thought occurred to me, I was startled by a sudden thud, the sound of a heavy object being moved. The woman had turned her body toward the camera. And there, in her lap, was the head of a man looking upward, a corpse slumped over.

I am not sure how best to describe what I felt at that moment. It was like nothing I had ever experienced before, a breathless feeling, as if all the blood in my body had been drained, and my consciousness began to dim; the feeling had gone far beyond fear, reducing me to an insensate numbness that was close to ecstasy ... I knew that the body was a corpse not only because the eyes were open wide despite his prone position, but because the collar had been torn from the elegant tails he wore, and his neck was wrapped tightly in a piece of crimson silk crepe that looked like a woman's undergirdle. His hands were outstretched, as if caught in the throes of death reaching out for his soul as it escaped his body, and had reached the collar-piece of the woman's kimono, which was covered in a gaudy embroidered image of wisteria flowers the color of celadon. She had inserted her hands in the corpse's armpits, and twisted her body around to reposition it as it lay there like a dead tuna. But she was only able to move the torso. The rest of the body, from the fat waist swelling up like a white cummerbund-wrapped hill and downward, remained in the same position, such that the body was now jackknifed, like a recumbent letter "V." Her delicate arms did not look up to the task of moving that ponderous belly— or so one would think from the sight of this dead man. He was quite obese despite having a relatively small frame. I could not see his face very clearly, but I could see enough from the side to guess that he was ugly and around thirty, with a low nose, a protruding forehead and skin flushed red as if he were drunk.

Now that things had come to this point I was obliged to admit that Sonomura's insane prediction had turned out to be exactly right. The woman's obi was covered in a silver fish-scale motif, and as I looked more closely at the dead man's head lying on it, I noticed that his hair, just as Sonomura had predicted, was parted cleanly in the middle and covered in gleaming hair oil.

It was not only the man's dead body that had now been revealed to me, but as the woman looked down and gazed at the face of the corpse in her lap, her full-cheeked, statuesque profile also came into my field of vision. She seemed to glory in the way the electric light hanging from the ceiling lit up her beautiful skin. It was bright as the midday sun and rendered every part of her perfectly visible without a speck of shadow; you could count each one of her eyelashes as they extended to the edge of her face, straight as the teeth of a comb. The elegance of the soft eyelids covering her downturned eyes; the sheer height and striking lines of the nose below them; the conspicuous crimson of her noble lips etched between two lovely cheeks; the taut but gentle line of her jaw as it fell smoothly from the corner of her lower lip and stretched toward the nape of her long neck—my heart stood still as I devoured each of these sights in turn.

That she looked this beautiful no doubt had something to do with the abnormality of the scene being played out in this room. But even accounting for that effect, she was no ordinary beauty. I have recently joined the ranks of those who have tired of the typically Japanese, geisha-style beauty, although hers was not necessarily one of those thin, high-cheeked "squash seed" style faces of the women you see in Edo-era picture books. It was a face that uncannily combined flirtatiousness and haughty pride: a youthful, plump roundness softly enveloping perfect eyes and a nose stationed icily in the center.

If one were to go looking for imperfections in her face, there were a few: the sharp widow's peak on her forehead added a note of coarseness to an otherwise harmonious countenance, a slight cloud of meanness and short-temperedness seemed to hover in the space between the too-thick eyebrows as they crowded in from left and right, and those bitter creases around her mouth, tightly closed as if she were feeling nauseous after swallowing some bitter potion meant to prevent even a small leakage of kindness—such were the only flaws to be found. And yet these very imperfections seemed to fit the freakish scene rather vividly, to intensify her beauty and make it only more bewitching.

It looked like we had gotten our first glimpse inside the room just after the man was killed. Or, indeed, the fellow may have been breathing his last just as I brought my eye to the knothole. The man with the crewcut leaning against the wall and this woman were no doubt still in a daze as the reality of the crime they had committed slowly dawned on them.

"Hey Sister! Are we good, or what?" said the man with the crew-cut, finally returning to his senses, blinking quickly and speaking in a low whisper.

"Oh yes, we are very good!... It's time for you to take the picture now!" said the woman, with a cold laugh, glinting like the flash of a razor blade. Her eyes, which had been cast down until then, were suddenly wide open and looking upward, and I understood for the first time the bottomless depths of the light they emitted, like a silent current from some underground spring, weirdly calm, and black as a slab of obsidian.

"Ok, then. I need you to move a little further back."

At these words the two of them sprang into action. The women hauled the corpse up and dragged it next to the tub on the right, and then sat up again, facing forward. The man went back to the camera, pointed the lens at the woman, and began busily adjusting the focus. As he did this, the woman raised her eyebrows—making her look even more threatening—and put all her energy into pinioning the corpse with its drumlike belly to prevent it from sliding off her lap. She had raised the torso up higher than before, so that the top of the head just grazed the tip of her chin, its face turned haplessly upward. It was clear, from all of this, that what they wanted to photograph was not the alluring figure of the woman in her squashed Shimada, but the dead face of this man who had just been cruelly strangled.

"Can you lift him up more? The fat gut is in the way and I can't get a good shot of the face."

"But he's so heavy! I can't lift him another inch! It really is a huge belly isn't it? He weighed close to 170 pounds, you know!"

As they chatted casually, the man slid a photographic plate into the camera and removed the lens cover. The exposure was long and it took some time before he replaced the cover, during which the corpse in black tails lay there with its arms splayed out like a frog's, its neck lolling to the left, and its extremities limply drooping like a screaming baby being lifted into its mother's arms. Needless to say, the scrap of silk crepe wrapped around the man's neck hung limply there.

"The exposure is finished. We're all set."

When the man said this, the woman let out a sigh of relief, letting the corpse roll over on its side; she then pulled a small hand mirror out of her obi—concerned even at a moment like this that her coiffure might collapse—outspread her ivory-colored hands bedecked with diamonds and pearls, and administered two or three careful pats to her Shimada hairdo.

The man went to the kitchen entrance on the other side of the reed blinds where I could hear him operating a faucet, and then came the sound of water pouring into a bucket or some other receptacle. Soon after this, my nose was assailed with a strange chemical odor I had never smelled before, like something from a doctor's pharmacy. At first, I thought the man was developing the photograph he had just taken. But the odor was too strange and unfamiliar. It brought tears to my eyes when I smelled it; something like smoldering sulphur.

The man emerged from the shadows of the blinds holding a test tube in each hand.

"I think I have the mixture where it needs to be. How does it look to you? Is this the right color?"

As he said this, he stood directly under the glass bulb, swishing some liquid around inside each test tube before letting it settle.

Having only the vaguest knowledge of chemistry I, unfortunately, had no idea what sort of chemicals were inside the two test tubes, but there was no question that it was the source of the strange odor. The liquid in the man's right hand was of a light purplish color, while the fluid in his left was a clear peppermint green.

Shot through with the bright light of bulb, they sparkled brilliantly and made for a truly beautiful sight.

"Oh my! What gorgeous colors. They look like amethysts and emeralds! With colors like that we will be fine!"

The woman laughed sweetly as she said this. It was not the ghastly cackle from earlier, but more of a flowery laugh, with a wide-open mouth and no sound. A gold filling on the upper-right canine and a protruding tooth on the left made the lovely smile even more charming.

"They are stunning, aren't they? With colors like these who could guess how frightening these chemicals are?"

The man brought the glass tubes up above his eye level and was gazing at them, enraptured.

"It's beautiful *because* it's frightening, silly! Don't they say that demons are just as beautiful as gods?"

"Yes, and it's all we need. Once we dissolve him with this chemical there won't be a trace left of him. Not a shred of evidence ..."

The man said this as if speaking to himself, and then suddenly he strode toward the tub and calmly began to pour the liquid from the tubes into it, drop by drop, after which he returned to the kitchen and carried five or six bucketfulls of water to the tub until it was full to the brim.

What did he do next? What did he dissolve with that chemical? And what ingredients went into making those chemicals that looked like precious jewels and gave off that strange sulfurous smell? Do such chemicals really exist in the world? — even now, thinking back on it, the whole thing seems like a dream.

Not long after, the man said, "If we leave it like this, he'll be mostly dissolved by morning."

To which the woman replied, "He's fat. It won't be like before with Matsumura-san. It'll take a while before the whole body is gone."

The woman spoke these words with perfect composure, after the two of them had hauled the corpse up—still wearing the tails—and sloshed it into the tub brimming with the chemical mixture.

While she worked on pickling the corpse the woman had dashingly tucked up her kimono sleeves and tied them in place with a cord, exposing her two white arms. Now that she had completed this task she made no move to untie the cord, but stood there with both hands resting on the edge of the tub, staring intently at the surface of the water like Salome watching Jokanaann. On her left arm, about seven or eight inches above her wrist, I could clearly make out a gold armband in the shape of a snake with ruby eyes coiled twice around the alabaster column of her arm.

The dissolution of the man's body in the chemical bath, however, was not so clearly visible to me. As I indicated earlier, the tub was in the shape of a Western-style bathtub and quite tall, so all I could see was the man's potbelly protruding slightly above the surface and the boiling bubbles of foam that crowded around it.

"How splendid! The chemicals are doing a fine job today aren't they? They are making quick work of that fat gut! At this pace it will be gone long before tomorrow morning."

Hearing the man with the crewcut say this, I had a closer look and saw that the belly was indeed shrinking steadily like a deflating balloon, until finally the edge of the white waistcoat had completely sunk into the liquid beneath.

"That went swimmingly don't you think? What do you say we worry about the rest tomorrow and get some sleep."

The woman collapsed onto the tatami with a disappointed air, and put a match to a gold-tipped cigarette she pulled out of her kimono sleeve.

The man with the crewcut obligingly brought out an extravagantly luxurious set of bedding from the closet next to the veranda and spread it out in the middle of the floor. It consisted of two thick cotton futons, the lower one covered with black velvet resembling the pelt of a cat and the upper one with white silk damask. There was also a set of loose linen pajamas covered in light-pink roses in a chintz pattern. They appeared to be cool on the skin. Once he had spread out her bedding, the man moved to the next room where he seemed to be putting out his own.

The woman changed into a white *habutae* silk night dress. She stepped over to the soft futons, which gave way under her feet like a bog or a swamp. And then, like the *yuki-onna* of ancient legends, she stood upright, raised her hand to the ceiling, and switched off the light.

If the woman had not turned off the light at that moment, without a doubt we would have remained there all night with our eyes glued to the knotholes, having forgotten the dangerous position we were in, our souls held captive by the scene playing out in front of us. Now that the room was suddenly dark, I at last regained consciousness of the fact that I had been crouching at the back of this cramped alleyway for an hour. In fact, if truth be told, we kept standing there next to the window half dazed even after the light went out, as if expecting something else to happen.

My first concern, as I emerged from this dreamlike state, was how on earth we would manage to escape this alley without them hearing our footsteps. The space between the eaves was barely wide enough for one person to pass, and one bang of the shoe was bound to give us away. The very fact that I had been able to hear every word the two of them whispered to each other was clear evidence of our extreme proximity. If they were ever to know that we had witnessed their crime what would our fate be? What we had seen tonight left no doubt as to how bold they were in the commission of crimes, of the ingenious means they had at their disposal, how carefully they planned their actions, and how relentlessly they pursued them. Even if we did manage to escape tonight without mishap, if they ever set their sights on us, our lives would be in mortal danger. It was far too easy to imagine the same fate befalling us as the man in the black tails, his limbs dissolving away in the vat of chemicals. At the very least, we had to recognize this danger, and live our lives with extreme caution from now on. As the full reality of this dawned on us, we realized that we had to take the utmost care not to leave this place in a careless fashion.

The situation was desperate. But I quickly determined that the best way out was to wait patiently for twenty or thirty minutes until they fell asleep, and then to make a quiet retreat. Sonomura was standing further in and could not leave until I did. But he seemed to have reached the same conclusion as me. He stood there unmoving, with bated breath, and presently reached out and squeezed my right hand, as if to implore me not to make any rash or sudden moves.

Given the circumstances, it is something of a miracle that Sonomura and I were able to maintain this level of discernment and composure. It was surprising enough that our limbs continued to support us despite shaking so much from fear that we could not keep our teeth clenched. If that shaking had been just a little stronger, if my chest, arms, and hips had jittered slightly more, could we have avoided making even the sound of a needle dropping? Coward that I am in most instances, I could only marvel at this miraculous show of courage when faced with this life-and-death situation.

But fortunately, we didn't have to stand there for much longer. Scarcely ten minutes after the woman put out the light we heard, from inside the room—what an utterly audacious pair they were!—the sound of the woman breathing deep in slumber, and the man with the crewcut snoring peacefully next door. I knew then our lives had been spared. I crept on tiptoe out of the alley.

When I had made it around to the front, Sonomura slapped me on the back, and said, "Wait up there! I still have to show you the fish-scale mark!... Look over there. You will find a white triangular mark."

Sonomura pointed to a space just under the eaves of the house. And sure enough, next to the nameplate was a fish-scale mark written in chalk, conspicuous enough to be visible at night.

The more I thought about it, the more the whole affair seemed mysterious, as if some phantom were at work. And yet even for a mystery it was too mysterious; and the lights were too bright for phantoms. I had witnessed it all with my own eyes, but I could not banish the thought that I had somehow been deceived.

"If we had arrived just two or three minutes earlier we would have seen it starting from the moment when they killed him. What a shame," said Sonomura.

Without even realizing it, the two of us had soon retraced the windy streets to Ningyō-chō, and then on to Edobashi. I felt a wet and clammy wind cool my face. The sky began half-clear, but at some point the stars disappeared behind a sheet of clouds, like the cotton in an old futon, ready to spill out at any moment.

"Sonomura! Lower your voice, would you? This is not a subject to discuss in the open like this! And where are we heading anyway? Whose place do we go back to? If we keep traipsing around like this in the middle of the night we could very well be caught!"

My face contorted with anxiety as I lectured Sonomura. I was even more agitated than he was, and it seemed I was the one now whose mind was showing signs of aberration.

"Caught? Of course we won't be caught! You worry needlessly. Do you seriously believe that this crime will be reported in tomorrow's newspapers and known to all the world? Think how ingenious their methods were! Surely you can see that they are far too clever to leave any detectable traces of what they have done! The man they killed will be declared a missing person; the police will search for him for a time, find nothing, and before long it will all be forgotten. I have no doubt about that. So even if we were somehow in collusion with them, our crime would never be exposed to the public glare. And it's not the glare of society that worries me, it's theirs! If that man and that woman had seen us, we would be done for—well and truly! That prospect was infinitely more frightening. Luckily, however, we managed to escape without being seen, so we are perfectly safe. We have nothing to worry about. And now that our lives are no longer in danger, there are some things I would like to do."

"What else is there to do? We have already seen the conclusion of tonight's events, have we not?"

Having failed to grasp the meaning of Sonomura's words I peered suspiciously at the smile on his face.

"Oh, it is very far from over. The fun has only just begun. I'll take advantage of their not having seen us before to play the idiot and approach them. Just wait and see how they react!"

"Please put that dangerous idea out of your head at once! I am already more than sufficiently convinced of your skills as a detective."

I was less shocked by this preposterous plan than I was simply angry with him.

"The sleuthing is over, but now we have other work to do.... I'll explain the rest in the car ride home. It's late, so you should stay at my place tonight."

As he said this, he hailed a taxi that was hurtling toward us from the direction of Uogashi.

The automobile took us past the Central Post Office to the edge of Nihonbashi, straight along the streetcar tracks of the deserted nighttime boulevards.

"So as I was saying," said Sonomura, as he launched into his story, looking me straight in the face. Gradually he became more excited, and his pupils filled with an abnormal light. He may not have been completely insane, but there was no denying a certain madness in him. His nerves oscillated weirdly between dullness and overexcitement, and there was something pathological about the way his brain functioned with uncanny clarity in one moment only to revert to childlike ingenuousness in the next. It was no doubt this pathological quality in his brain that had allowed him to sense in advance the horrific events we had witnessed this evening.

"You'll understand well enough once I explain what I have in mind for later and how I plan to carry it out. But first, tell me what your feelings were as you watched the crime play itself out before our eyes earlier. Of course it was horrific. But was it only that? Aside from the horror, did you not experience, for example, any strange emotions in relation to the woman's actions or her appearance?"

Sonomura pressed me impatiently to answer.

But I was in far too grave a mood to consider questions like these. The scene had imprinted itself powerfully in my brain ... I knew I would never forget it as long as I lived, and each time it came back to me I felt as if a ghost had taken possession of me, and all I could do was gaze blankly in Sonomura's direction.

"You doubted my prediction until the moment you saw the room through the knothole yourself, did you not? You didn't believe we would actually witness a murder, did you? ..."

Sonomura kept on talking, paying no attention to my diminished state.

"You thought I had gone mad yesterday, and you followed me into that alleyway as if you were attending to a mental patient. I knew perfectly well that on the inside you found it all a colossal nuisance, but were just playing along for my sake. I knew you were treating me like a mental patient. Indeed, you may still think I'm mad. But whether I am mad or not, what we saw through that knothole is a fact that can no longer be put into doubt. Not even you can deny this. And since you, unlike I, were not mentally prepared to witness such a scene, it must have been even more shocking and horrific for you. At the very least, I believe I was able to observe the scene with greater detachment than you. I may have been no less surprised than you when the corpse on that woman's lap first came into our vision, but the reason for my surprise was completely different from yours ...

"When the woman had her back to us, I don't suppose you noticed that she had an object in her lap. You therefore could not guess what the woman and the man with the crewcut were doing. I, on the other hand, knew from very early on that a corpse lay in the shadow there. As I'm sure you also remember, in the beginning the woman was sitting so close to us that her body blocked the knothole. My own knothole, moreover, was a foot lower than yours, so that for some time all I could make out was the right side of the woman's back and shoulder, one portion of the wall opposite, and the side of the metal tub, but then the woman scooted forward on her buttocks about a yard. I believe you took your eye away from the knothole briefly at that moment, but I saw how the woman scrambled forward on her hips, the length of a single tatami mat. Of course because she moved away from us in a straight line, the object in the shadows in front of her was still not visible to us. But we were now able to take in the whole of her backside for the first time. The woman sat with her torso tilted slightly to the left, with both hands in her lap, as if she were working on a piece of needlework ... that's how it was, right? ... One look at her posture was enough for me to sense that she was cradling the head of a strangled man in her lap. It may not have been obvious at first, but that was not the posture of someone with an ordinary object in their lap. You may not have noticed, but her posture was somehow unnatural; her spine and hips stretched bolt upright and only her head faced downward. She had such an elegant and supple figure that her awkwardness was easy to overlook, but she was clearly holding something extremely heavy and putting all her strength into supporting its weight. Also, because she was concentrating most of her strength in her arms, I could clearly see a slight but noticeable shaking caused by the tensing of her muscles in both shoulders and all the way down her back. These tremors even gave rise, from time to time, to large undulating waves along the length of her kimono sleeves. I think the woman had approached the dead man, hauled his upper body into her lap and, while checking to see if he had really stopped breathing, gave his neck one last squeeze to be certain. This is the only way to explain her movements. She was flexing both arms so hard because she was pulling the piece of silk crepe tight around his neck. I had by this point already guessed there was a corpse in the woman's shadow, so I was not surprised when it eventually did come into our view. What did surprise me was the woman's beauty. Until then, my attention had been focused exclusively on the crime being committed so I was not prepared for the beauty of that face.

"Yes, even I can recognize that she was an attractive woman."

I was beginning to find this quite irritating, and my tone grew harsh. "One can recognize it, but isn't it strange for you of all people to go on and on about it like this. Yes, she was quite a beauty, but there are any number of women like her among the top class of geisha. You yourself must have encountered women like her in the days when you frequented the geisha houses in Shimbashi and Akasaka."

I meant for this to be ironic. Sonomura had recently declared that there was no such thing as a beautiful geisha, peremptorily ceased visiting the entertainment districts, and had become fixated instead on Western moving pictures. When he felt the need for a woman he would head off to a cheap teahouse in the Yoshiwara or a brothel in Asakusa Rokku to satisfy his sexual desire in the most expedient way possible. Despite having at one time come close to blowing his entire inheritance on geisha, he now harbored an extreme antipathy toward them, and often announced in my presence that "the women in the brothels of Asakusa are more beautiful than the lot of them!" For someone whose tastes had become as decadent as his, there was something incongruous in his praise for the woman tonight.

"True enough!" he said. "If it's looks alone we are talking about, yes, there are any number of equally beautiful women in Shimbashi and Akasaka ... but I am not convinced that this woman is a geisha at all."

Sonomura had panicked and was now clearly grasping at straws.

"It seems perfectly reasonable to me to assume that a woman in a squashed Shimada and dressed like that is a geisha. At the very least one could say that her kind of beauty is typical of a geisha."

"Would you be so kind as to shut your mouth for a moment and listen to what I have to say? Yes, it is true that, on the basis of her style and her taste in clothing, she would appear to be a geisha. The face too, I grant you, is the type of face one often sees on picture postcards of geisha. But did you not notice the strange expression hovering around those thick eyelashes—that frightful expression of cruelty and strength like that of a wild animal? What did you think of the cold cruelty of her lips, the bottomless cunning inscribed in the lines and colors of her face, somehow tinged at the same time with the melancholic luster of regret? Could there ever be a geisha with a beauty as sick as that? There are no doubt any number of women whose features would rival hers. But what geisha's beauty has a depth like that? What say you, my friend? Do you not agree?"

"I do not."

My response was extremely cool.

"Yes, the face was beautiful. But it was beautiful in a perfectly typical way. You have to consider the context. The woman was in the process of killing a man, for god's sake. Any human being engaged in such a wicked act will have a terrifying expression on their face. And it is only natural that the expression would take on added depth, and even a pathological cast. She was an extreme beauty to begin with, so the sick quality was accentuated and gave her a ghoulish appearance. But if you were to encounter that same woman in an ordinary geisha house, I bet you couldn't pick her out of a group of geisha!…"

At some point during this discussion the car arrived at Sonomura's house by Shiba Park.

It was close to four in the morning, and the short summer night was beginning to whiten toward dawn, but neither of us felt like resting, even after this long night of chasing about town. Just as we had done yesterday, we soon found ourselves seated on the sofa in his study raising glasses of brandy, spouting cigarette smoke, engaged enthusiastically in discussion.

"In any case, I don't see why you're so focused on the woman's beauty. The nature of the crime itself is far more baffling, if you ask me."

At this, Sonomura knocked back the snifter of brandy he was holding to his lips, set it on the table, and declared, "I want to get closer to that woman." He pronounced these words in a low whisper with a mixture of desperation and hesitancy, followed by a long sigh.

"It's started again, hasn't it? Your sickness."

No sooner had this thought occurred to me than I found myself saying it out loud.

"You won't hear any complaints from me if you think twice before putting this reckless plan into action. If you go near that woman, what's to stop you from ending like the man in the black tails? I know you have your eccentricities, but surely the desire to be strangled and pickled are not among them? Unless of course you no longer care to live, in which case you may as well see how close to her you can get."

"There is no reason to think just getting close to her will be fatal. If I take care from the start, I'll be fine! And besides, as I said earlier, she has no idea that we know her secret, so she has no reason to kill me. That's what makes it so exciting!"

"Something really is the matter with you! You may not be mad, but you do have a very severe case of neurasthenia. Please proceed with care, I beg you!"

"Thank you for these words of caution. I do appreciate them. But I must ask you to allow me to act as I see fit. Recently I have somehow lost interest in an ordinary life, and am no longer at home in my own skin. I have begun to feel that without some bizarre stimulus I cannot go on living. In fact, it's only seeing things like what we saw tonight that prevents me from going insane from sheer monotony."

As he said these words, Sonomura put back glass after glass of brandy, as if toasting himself and his madness. He was fond of alcohol, even slightly addicted to it, such that his fingertips would tremble when he was sober. But once the alcohol hit his bloodstream, his face would turn pale, his eyes would take on a cavernous expression, and a queer calm would overtake him.

"If you feel confident you won't be in danger of being killed, I suppose there is no harm in approaching her.... But how exactly will you get near her? What do you know about her position, her situation? She may be in the geisha business after all, but she is no ordinary geisha. Why did she kill that man? How did she obtain those horrific chemicals? And what is her relation to the man with the crewcut? It would be safer to get the answers to these questions before you approach her. Please take this much of my advice, I'm begging you."

I had started to become seriously worried about Sonomura.

He let out a loud guffaw.

"I am many steps ahead of you. I have a good notion of just what kind of people that woman and the man with the crewcut are. Even as I speak to you now I am carefully considering what method and what occasion I should employ to make my approach seem most natural. If you are right and she is a geisha it will be simple enough to approach her. But I don't believe she is."

"I myself never claimed for certain that she's a geisha. I simply noted that there are not many women who look like her and who are not geisha. My interpretation only goes that far. But do tell me, my good man, if she isn't a geisha, what sort of woman do you think she is? In fact, please say more than that. What was the motive of the murder? Why photograph the corpse? Why dissolve it in that chemical bath? And what chemicals did they use? If you have answers to any of these questions please enlighten me! I am quite baffled by the whole thing myself, but I stopped myself from asking until now."

I did worry that by posing all of these questions I might cause his already overheated brain to spin out in even stranger directions. And yet the sight of the crime had stimulated my curiosity to such an extent that I could not prevent myself from asking these questions.

"There is a great deal that I do not understand myself. But let me tell you what I have been able to observe ..." He began to explain, point by point, in the tone of a teacher patiently instructing a student.

"The fact is that I myself am still in the process of solving these mysteries and have yet to arrive at clear answers to all of them, but one thing I am certain of is that the woman is not a geisha. When I saw her in the cinema she wore her hair in a pompadour. And on her left hand, with which I saw her write those *katakana* characters, she was not wearing the rings we saw her in tonight. And you recall the sweet, floral perfume of her kimono that assailed our nostrils through the knothole. I was even closer to her at the cinema the other night, and my sense of smell is very acute, but I picked up no scent at all. I am not suggesting that these were two different women. A person who is careful enough to dissolve a body in acid so as not to leave the slightest trace of a murder would hardly delegate such an important job to someone else. The woman on that evening was in a crucial communication with the man in the crew-cut, using both *katakana* and a cryptographic code, so she must indeed have been the same woman we saw tonight. This would suggest, then, that she is someone who dresses and accessorizes differently depending on the day. Add to this the possibility that she is a habitual criminal, and she will have even more use for disguises. Depending on the circumstances, she might well put her hair in a squashed Shimada and play the role of a geisha on one day, and then switch to a pompadour in the manner of a schoolgirl the next. If she really were a geisha, shouldn't she have been wearing rings and perfume that night at the theater as well? And what's more, the fragrance on her kimono this evening was not that of a perfume worn by a geisha ...

"Do you know what that smell was? ... It was not perfume at all. It was old-fashioned agarwood incense. The woman had treated her kimono with incense smoke. Think about it, how many geisha do you know who burn incense into their clothing? The woman is clearly an eccentric. And if you want more evidence, did you see that splendid gold armband when she tucked up her sleeves to haul the body? It was far too garish and gaudy for a normal geisha to wear. Combine that armband with the squashed Shimada, and the incense-infused clothing, and it makes for quite a bizarre and incongruous spectacle! Whatever else you want to say about her, this is clearly a woman who revels in eccentric behavior. You also have to take into consideration the fact that the man she killed was wearing tails. Think how striking and conspicuous such an outfit was in those circumstances. It adds yet another twist to the labyrinth of this incident if you consider the strange pairing of a geisha with a man in tails. And remember what she said to the man with the crewcut?—'Frightening things are always beautiful,' and 'Demons are as beautiful as the gods,' or some such. A bit too brazen for a geisha, I would say. And then there is the cipher she used to write that message—how many geisha are able to write in secret codes using English? It may not be completely beyond the realm of the imagination that a geisha should be so educated, but if there were such a geisha combining beauty and intelligence to such a degree, would you and I not have heard of her before? And how, in any case, could a geisha get her hands on such a frightful chemical? She even knew how to prepare it; we saw her giving instructions to the man with the crewcut, did we not?... For these reasons I do not believe she's a geisha. But there is one more piece of evidence to clinch my hypothesis. When she put the corpse into the chemical bath she said, 'He's fat. It won't be like before with Matsumura-san. It'll take a while before the whole body is gone.' You remember her saying that, no doubt ... But does this name 'Matsumura' call anything to mind?"

"Yes I do recall her mentioning the name 'Matsumura.' But I don't have a clue who it is. Do you?"

"You may recall a while ago—two months ago to be exact—a newspaper article announcing that a certain Viscount Matsumura had gone missing?"

"Oh yes! The memory is dim, but I think I do recall reading
something to that effect."

"The article appeared in the morning paper and in the previous
evening paper, along with a photograph of the man in question.
The evening version included quite a lot of detail, as well as in-
terviews with family members. Apparently the viscount had just
returned from a tour of Europe and America a week before he went
missing. He had become depressed abroad, shutting himself up in
his home, and refusing to see anyone upon his return to Tokyo.
Then one day he announced that he felt too cooped up, and left
his estate, saying he would take a trip somewhere and be gone for a
month, and then disappeared.

"The viscount let it be known that he would travel to Kyoto,
then on to Nara, and finally to the Dōgo hot spring on the island
of Shikoku. One of his footmen saw him off at Tokyo Station and
witnessed him purchasing a ticket and then boarding a train for
Kyoto. The family speculated that he had suffered a breakdown
on the trip and committed suicide. He brought a large amount of
cash with him and they discovered no will, so it may not have been
a premeditated suicide. He may simply have hit upon the idea while
traveling. Or so they said. For ten days the Matsumura family ran
an ad with the viscount's portrait, offering a reward for information
leading to his discovery. But no meaningful clues surfaced. On the
morning after his departure from Tokyo, there was one person who
claimed to have seen a young gentleman resembling the portrait
of the viscount leaving the platform at Shichijō Station in Kyoto
with a young aristocratic-looking woman in tow. According to the
footman, his master had lived in total seclusion since his return
from Europe and had no close friends in society. And of course he
had never set foot in the pleasure districts, so the story of his being
seen with a young aristocratic-looking woman simply did not hold

water. Two months have now passed with no news of the viscount and no report either that his corpse has been found. No one knows if he is dead or alive. When I read the story in the paper I paid little attention, but when I heard the woman say 'Matsumura-san' earlier, I recalled it immediately. Was the Matsumura she murdered not this missing viscount? It had to be him. It must be; I feel quite certain of it … What do you say, my good man? Just think about it for a moment. The viscount disappeared somewhere between Tokyo and Kyoto. If something had happened to him on the train before it reached Kyoto, we would have heard about it. This suggests that whatever happened to him happened after his arrival in Kyoto. Aside from the person who claimed to see him at Shichijō station, he was not spotted at any other station or inn, which suggests that he must have committed suicide or was murdered somewhere in Kyoto. But whether suicide or homicide, most methods would have yielded a corpse to be discovered … So, this is what I think. The woman pointed to the man in tails and said, 'He's fat. It won't be like before with Matsumura-san.' So this Matsumura who she killed must have been thin. I've seen a photograph of Viscount Matsumura and he was indeed thin as a rail.

"And the woman made a point of adding the honorific -*san* when she spoke of Matsumura. Calling him 'Matsumura-san,' suggests not only that she wasn't particularly intimate with him, but also that she respected him in some way. If you speak about someone you don't know very well it's common enough just to use their name unadorned with -*san*. But if the person in question is well known in society circles, or an aristocrat, most people would append a -*san* to the name. So the fact that the woman referred to 'Matsumura-san' would suggest that he was a member of the peerage, and that she was not particularly close to him. If the man was her husband, or lover, or in some other similarly intimate relation to her, she would not take the trouble of adding -*san* to the bugger's name when she killed him! Something like 'that damned Matsumura' or just 'that bastard!' would be the more natural appellation. It might be hasty of me to hypothesize based on this evidence alone that the Matsumura the woman murdered and Viscount Matsumura are one and the same person. But there is one additional fact that strengthens my theory even further: the rumor that the viscount was seen together with a young aristocratic-looking woman disembarking at Shichijō Station. The footman negates the rumor by claiming that the viscount had no relations with women of any sort. But what if he had met her on the train and then had become close to her? Unlikely, perhaps, given the viscount's reputation for shyness. But if the woman were sufficiently cunning, if she made a target of the viscount and employed her wiles to seduce him, and if she were not unattractive to boot, who is to say that he might not be susceptible to her approaches? We know that he had a large amount of cash with him, so perhaps the woman had pursued him from Tokyo with the intention of taking it off his hands.... When I think about it this way I feel quite certain that the young aristocratic-looking woman was none other than the woman we saw last night, that she murdered the viscount somewhere in Kyoto, after which she dissolved his body in that chemical bath..."

"So you think this woman is some kind of railway robber?"

"Yes, I believe so. Something like that ... the fact that the viscount is still missing is best explained by the assumption that this Matsumura fellow who she killed and dissolved in acid was the viscount. If it's true that she had never met the viscount before, it makes sense that she killed him purely for the money he was carrying. So yes, I think she is a railway robber. But no ordinary one. I suspect she is a member of a large-scale criminal operation and she committed this crime in her spare time. She committed the same kind of murder in Tokyo and the Kansai region. No doubt there was another house in Kyoto outfitted with the same chemicals and Western-style bathtub. I will wager there is a whole gang of these villains shuttling back and forth on the Tōkaidō, passing messages in that secret cipher and perpetrating all manner of horrific crimes, one after another."

"The more you talk, the more convinced I am that your observations are spot on. Do you suppose the man in tails she killed tonight was also a member of the aristocracy?"

I continued to pose questions like this to Sonomura. I must confess that after a certain point I had found myself in awe of his prowess as a detective and compelled to ask for his confirmation of every point.

"No, I don't think he was an aristocrat. I believe today's murder was quite different from the Viscount Matsumura's."

As he said this Sonomura stood up and opened the east-facing window of his Western-style home, letting in the refreshing morning air to cool off the room, which had grown muggy and clouded with cigarette smoke.

"I have reason to believe that the man was a member of their organization." Sonomura spoke these words, returned to his chair, and looked hard at my face as my eyes blinked in disbelief.

"From the way he acted when I saw him at the cinema, the man must have been the woman's lover or husband. You may think he was an aristocrat because he was wearing tails. But would an aristocrat be seen wearing tails in a grungy place at the back of an alleyway? It's more likely that he was a criminal posing as an aristocrat who had just returned home. If the man was the woman's lover, this is the only explanation that makes sense. Do you remember when she said, 'It really is a huge belly isn't it? He weighed close to 170 pounds, you know!' I think that line, 'He weighed close to

170 pounds, you know!' is more than we need to understand the relationship between these two people."

"I have to agree with your observation here as well. So do you imagine the woman was having an affair with the man with the crewcut and that they killed this other fellow to get him out of the way?"

"Well, it does seem like that's where this is all heading. But there is also evidence to the contrary. You noticed that after they put the body into the tub the man with the crewcut put the woman's bedding out first and then laid out his own in the room next door. Also, the man was always following her orders and calling her 'Sister.' This doesn't make them sound like a couple who are romantically involved. And then there is the matter of the photograph. Why take a photograph of the body when they went so far as to dissolve it in acid in order to get rid of the evidence? The image of a man one has murdered with one's own hands is frightening enough in dreams, so why keep a photo of him? In any case, this was a very strange murder, and the reason for it may be lurking where we least expect to find it."

"Lurking somewhere unexpected? Please elaborate."

"For example—and this is based on my own idiosyncratic deductions—but let's say that woman had some kind of sexual abnormality that made her experience a kind of secret pleasure in killing people. Perhaps she has a habit of killing people just because she wants to and not out of any necessity. If we look closely at her behavior this is not difficult to imagine. Do you follow? At first the viscount was killed as a result of coming into her orbit. Of course the motive may have had to do with getting rid of the evidence of the theft. But then again, the money the viscount had with him was just his traveling expenses—let's say ¥1,000 at the most. There ought to have been a way to steal that amount of money without killing anyone. She could have fed him a sleeping pill, or had one of her henchmen do it. And a woman like her has any number of ways to cover her tracks. And yet, she kills him, and not in any ordinary way. She goes through all the trouble of luring him into Kyoto and taking him to their lair, where she murders him and dissolves his body in acid. This is quite a cumbersome method of murder. The murder last night was even more bizarre. There was no money involved, and it wasn't a crime of passion. The man in tails died meaninglessly, and they went to considerable trouble to commemorate it in a photograph. In this single incident, it is clear that the murder was the result of the woman's profligacy and her pathological predilections. I wouldn't be surprised if the viscount had also gotten his picture taken. In fact I imagine she has killed any number of men with this method and has a whole collection of photos of their corpses. No doubt she takes some brutal satisfaction from the sight of the dead faces of the countless men who lost their lives after being seduced by her. Who's to say, in any case, that a woman with such a sexual perversion doesn't exist somewhere in the world?..."

"I too can imagine that such a woman exists somewhere. But there must be some other reason why the man in tails had to be sacrificed to her desire. Even if she is as perverted as you claim, she would not choose just any man to be her victim. Why is it, for example, that she killed the man in tails and not the one with the crewcut?"

"That's easy ... the man in tails was not only her lover, he was also the leader of the criminal gang. She wanted to kill someone superior to her, and someone unexpected. The man with the crewcut was one of their underlings. She could have killed him easily at any moment. No point in sacrificing someone like that. Clearly she targeted Viscount Matsumura because of his social status as an aristocrat. This made it interesting and stimulated her curiosity. And killing the leader of her gang came with the benefit that she would be able to take over as leader in his place. You saw how faithfully the man with the crewcut obeyed the orders of his new female boss."

"I see," I said, utterly convinced by now of Sonomura's explanations. "When you interpret it this way the mystery does seem to unravel. It all boils down to the fact that the woman is a cruel murderer."

"A cruel murderer ... yes, that's right. And she is also a beautiful sorceress. And yet to me her wickedness seems somehow abstract. It is completely eclipsed by her beauty. As I recall the scene from last night, all I can think of is what a tremendously beautiful monster she is, so ravishing—as to seem otherworldly. What we witnessed through the knotholes last night was the scene of ghastly murder, and yet it's left me with no especially horrifying impression or unpleasant memory. A man was murdered, but there was not a drop of blood in sight, not a moment's struggle, not even any faint moaning. It was a quiet, seductive sort of crime, carried out as gently as a lover's whisper. I felt no stirring of conscience, and found myself transfixed by the sheer beauty of what seemed to flicker like a bright and colorful painting before my eyes. When the woman said 'frightening things are always beautiful,' and 'demons are as beautiful as the gods,' the words sounded to me like they were describing not just those gemlike test tubes, but the woman herself. She is a heroine ripped from the pages of a detective novel, a devil incarnate; a demon who has long been nesting in the fantasy world inside my head. She is the fantasy I have longed for, now manifested in the real world and come to comfort me in my loneliness. I believe she has come into existence for my sake alone. I can even imagine that the crime we witnessed last night was staged especially for my benefit. I must see her, even if it means risking my life. I will put all of my efforts into finding her and being near her ... I appreciate your concern, but I ask you to keep it to yourself and allow me to do as I must. As I said before, my goal is not to expose this woman's secrets. I am in love with her. Or perhaps it would be more accurate to say: I worship her."

As he said this, Sonomura leaned back in his chair, placed his hands on the back of his head, closed his eyes, and for some time seemed lost in his thoughts.

I had no words to remonstrate with someone so far gone. I lacked the energy, in any case, to utter a word, and leaned back in my own chair, remaining silent. At some point the alcohol in our blood had liquefied the fatigue that suffused our bodies and we felt pleasantly enveloped in cottony clouds of sleep. Somewhere in the depths of my half-slumbering consciousness the thought occurred to me that I could easily sleep for two or even three days without interruption....

I SPENT THE WHOLE DAY AFTER THE MURDER sleeping at Sonomura's house and finally returned home to Koishikawa late the following evening. My wife had been waiting anxiously for me to return, and as soon as she saw me she said, "Oh, do tell me, how is Sonomura-san? Has he gone mad after all?"

"He's not exactly mad. But he is extremely agitated."

"Well what was all that ruckus about last night? This crazy talk about a murder happening. What on earth was he going on about?"

"No point in trying to understand the words of someone who has lost his senses."

"But you two went to Suitengū after that, didn't you?"

This caught me a bit off guard, but I responded as casually as I could.

"Oh please! I humored him for a while and eventually got him back home. Who in their right mind would go to Suitengū in the middle of the night? If there had been a murder it would have been in the paper wouldn't it?

"I guess you're right. But I do wonder how he got such an idea into his head. Madness really is a strange thing, isn't it?"

My wife seemed satisfied with this explanation.

Back in my own bed after two days, I thought back over the

previous day's events. It was Sonomura's phone call the morning before, just as I was writing the manuscript I had promised my editor, that started the whole sequence of events. If it had all been a dream, this phone call was what connected the dreamworld with reality. After that, I had been drawn into the labyrinth. If Sonomura's madness had indeed infected me, it had started at that moment. Perhaps there had been some kind of misunderstanding that suddenly became real ... but where did the confusion start?

No matter how much I thought about it, I could not identify the exact spot where things took a turn. What I had seen the night before seemed utterly real. The murder that had taken place in the back streets of Suitengū just after one in the morning the previous night was a fact that I witnessed with my own eyes. Call me mad, but there was no way to deny it. Had Sonomura characterized and judged these facts more or less accurately? Was he right about the nature of the crime, about the woman, the man with the crewcut, and the man in tails? In the absence of convincing counterarguments on my part, I had no choice but to accept Sonomura's account.

These anxieties and doubts were with me for five or six days. I visited Sonomura's home several times, but he was always out. The person staying there told me with a suspicious look that Sonomura had been leaving early every morning looking like he had something to do, and didn't return until late at night. Exactly one week had passed when I finally found him at home. He was in fine spirits and came out to the entrance himself to greet me.

"Hello, my good man! You have chosen a perfect time to visit!"

He suddenly lowered his voice to a whisper, and spoke gleefully, directly in my ear.

"That woman is here, now, in my study!"

"That woman is …?"

These were the only words I could get out. He had caught up with her after all. Or perhaps she had caught up with him? And now he had the crazy notion of introducing me to her.

"Yes, that's right. That woman is here … I have spent the last five or six days prowling around Suitengū on the lookout for her, but I didn't expect I would get close to her so soon. I'll tell you the whole story later of how I managed to maneuver myself into her good graces. But why don't you come and meet her?"

I was still hesitating, but he laughed off my cowardice.

"Oh come and say hello, old boy! You are not in any danger now. It can't hurt to meet her!"

"There may be no immediate danger involved in a quick meeting in your study. But this could become the occasion for greater intimacy, and then …"

"What harm is there in getting close to her! Why, she and I are already fast friends!"

"You have your own eccentric reasons for befriending her, and there's no stopping you now anyway. But I prefer to avoid such strange relations."

"So you refuse to meet her even though I took the trouble to bring her here?"

"I am curious to meet her. But I'd like to avoid a formal introduction. The best would be if you could somehow show her to me while I watch from the shadows.… What do you say? There are no gaps to peek through in your study so it might work best if you brought her into your Japanese-style room, while I stand outside in the bushes and watch."

"Excellent! I'll bring her close to the veranda to make it easy for you to see her. Just crouch down behind that low wall there. You should be able to hear us talking without any problem. Of course, if at any point you do feel ready to meet her, I am happy to make introductions. Just send the maid in with a message."

"Ha ha ha! I thank you for that. But I don't suspect I will need to trouble the maid."

As I said this, I suddenly recalled something that had been bothering me and, grabbing Sonomura's hand, I said to him, imploringly, "You may have become friends with the woman now, but please tell me you have no plans to reveal to her that you and I are privy to her secret! You yourself may be ready to die over this, but I'll thank you not to drag me into it!"

"You may put your mind at ease. I feel the same way. She has no notion that we were watching her that night. And I certainly have no intention of telling her."

"That is very good to hear. But please do be extremely careful. Don't forget that it is our secret as much as hers. And you have no right to reveal it without my consent."

I was extremely concerned, and tried to look intimidating as I said these words, and admonished him against any ill-considered moves.

I crouched behind the low wall in the garden and spied on the woman once again that night, but there is no reason to describe that in detail here. I will add only that the woman was without a doubt the same woman I had seen on that frightening night, that she wore her hair long with bangs parted in the middle, making her look like an actress, that she was wearing the same armband as before, and that she was every bit as beautiful as she had appeared when I saw her through the knothole.

Sonomura had become quite close to her already; first at a billiard hall called the Seiyūken in Asakusa. She was famous for hitting a hundred balls in a row in games of four-ball billiards.*

"My life is a secret," she told him. "You must not breathe a word about me to anyone. If you can keep that promise, I am all yours."

And so she began her association with Sonomura, with his silence as the sole condition. Sonomura, for his part, watched carefully to see which of his theories about her proved correct. He pretended not to know her address or anything of her circumstances and met her every day and night in the bars, restaurants, and hotels of Tokyo. The previous day he had met her at Shimbashi Station for an overnight trip to a hot spring in Hakone, next to Mt. Fuji, from where they had just returned to his house next to Shiba Park.

---

* Four-ball billiards, "yotsu-dama," was the most popular form of billiards in early twentieth-century Japan. It is played with four balls on a table with no pockets. The object is to hit or "carom on" as many of the other three balls as one can in a single shot. As long as a player caroms on at least two balls, he or she shoots again. One hundred consecutive shots on the part of the woman would not have been much fun for her opponent.

AND SO IT WAS THAT SONOMURA AND EIKO — THIS is what she called herself—became closer with each passing day. He was rarely home when I visited, but I often saw them out for a drive, camped out in a box at the theater, or holding hands and strolling through the Ginza. She was dressed differently each time; now a silk crepe *yukata* with a *haori* jacket, now in manteau cloak and with her hair like an actress, and now in white linen and high heels. She looked consistently beautiful no matter what she wore, but her facial expressions made her seem a different person every day.

And then, one day—I think it was about a month after the two of them had become close—something happened that shocked me to the core. I discovered, quite by chance, that Sonomura had at some point entangled himself not only with Eiko, but also with the man with the crewcut. It was at the Mitsukoshi Department Store. I was there to attend an exhibition, when I saw Sonomura come bounding excitedly down the three-story staircase with both Eiko and the crewcut in tow. Sonomura seemed intent on avoiding me, and I found myself standing still with shock, and not inclined to say a word. The man with the crewcut was comically dressed in a university student's uniform, following the two of them around deferentially, like a houseboy waiting on his masters.

"Now that this fellow has come onto the scene there is no telling what might happen to Sonomura. This is no longer a situation I can ignore." As I said this to myself, I resolved to put a stop to Sonomura's nonsense once and for all. The next morning I paid him a visit at home. But there, an even greater surprise awaited me. The houseboy who greeted me at Sonomura's door was none other than the man with the crewcut himself.

Today he was wearing the typical student houseboy's uniform of an unlined kimono of Kurume indigo cotton and Kokura-style hakama trousers. When I asked if his master were at home he clasped both hands together in a show of cordiality and said, "Yes, he is in!" with a smile that was both ingratiating and repellent.

I found Sonomura in a foul mood, slumped over on the marble table in his study. Shutting the door behind me to prevent our voices from escaping, I strode briskly over to him.

"The man with the crewcut has insinuated himself into your own house Sonomura! What on earth are you thinking?"

I did not hold back in my interrogation. But Sonomura only mumbled "Aye," in reply and shot back a sideways glare, looking even more ill-disposed than before. Perhaps he was ashamed at being asked and was putting on a show of anger to hide his embarrassment.

"If you don't say anything what am I to think? It looks as if you have taken that fellow in as a houseboy. But perhaps I am wrong?"

"Nothing is settled for certain. But he says he can't pay his school fees so I'm allowing him to stay here for the time being."

It took some time before Sonomura replied, pronouncing the words wearily and grudgingly, like a cow chewing its cud.

"School fees? Do you mean to say the man is enrolled in a university somewhere?"

"He is studying in the College of Law."

"So he says, no doubt. But can you really credit him? Have you checked to see if he is really enrolled?"

I pressed him for an answer.

"I don't know if it's true or if it's a lie. But he walks around town wearing the uniform of a College of Law student. He's a relative of Eiko's. Her cousin, apparently. That's how he was introduced to me, in any case, and I am associating with him on that basis."

Sonomura spoke as if there were nothing at all out of the ordinary going on. But the very nonchalance of his answer radiated animosity toward me. My question had clearly irritated him. I sat there dumbfounded for a moment, and stared vaguely into his eyes. But soon I regained my composure and said to him in an encouraging tone, "Please do to try to get ahold of yourself, old boy!"

With this, I administered a good slap on his back.

"You can't possibly be serious! Surely you don't actually believe every word of what that woman and that man have to say?"

"Listen, Takahashi. If it's what they say, why not take them at their word? Why go snooping around to verify the tales they tell? We know what kind of people they are, so any association with them requires a certain level of awareness, and there is no way around that."

"But even without snooping, you and I both know how dangerous it is to be anywhere near those two. If you are in love with Eiko, I suppose you can't help being near her. But for god's sake, can't you at least keep your distance from that man?"

As I said these words, Sonomura looked to the side again and fell silent.

"My dear friend! I came here today in order to deliver one last warning. Perhaps I am sticking my nose where it doesn't belong, but when I saw you with that man the other day at the Mitsukoshi Department Store, I was so worried about you that I could not remain silent. If you still think of me as your only friend, please heed my advice and keep your distance from him!"

"I know perfectly well how dangerous he is. But Eiko has asked me to look after him ... I am no longer able to refuse anything to her..."

Sonomura spoke with bowed head and downcast eyes, as if pleading for mercy.

"That may be fine for you. But as I said to you the other day, one wrong move on your part and I am exposed to danger as well. This makes it impossible for me to remain silent. It may come to the point where I have no choice but to report them to the police. I suggest you be prepared for that!"

There was anger in my voice. But Sonomura was nonplussed, and said to me calmly, "Those two are far too clever to be tripped up in a police investigation, so the only result of turning them in will be to make them resent us. And if that happens, you'll be in more danger than ever ... You would be wise, my friend, to avoid that course of action. You really have nothing to worry about as things stand now. I don't want to die any more than you do, so you can count on me not to say anything stupid."

"So no matter what I say, you refuse to heed my warning. In that case I will naturally have to prioritize my own safety and stay away from you in the future. You were no doubt expecting this?"

"Well, there's nothing to be done about it now."

Sonomura exhibited no surprise at my words. He simply continued to cast sidelong glances in my direction ... he was willing to throw away his life for the love of a woman. How could the friendship of a single man begin to compare?... This is what the look in his eyes seemed to be saying.

"All right, then! I'll be going now. I have no more business in this house ..."

He made no effort to stop me as I said this. I beat a hasty retreat and he leaned languorously on his table, watching me go.

SO ENDED MY ASSOCIATION WITH SONOMURA.
Given how impetuous he was, I thought at some point he would
begin to feel lonely and come back to me full of apologies. Surely
he would come to regret having made me angry ... But soon a full
month had passed without a phone call or letter. It is true that the
situation at the time had made me angry. But in my heart I still felt
close to Sonomura, and his total silence began to worry me.

"What if Sonomura had been killed? Had he not met the same
fate as the man in tails? If not that, why had he cut off contact
with me for so long?" I could not stop worrying along these lines. I
was also curious for reasons beyond my friendship with Sonomura.
What had become of the woman who called herself "Eiko," and the
man with the crewcut? Had Sonomura been able to learn more
about their strange story?

As it happened, the long-awaited message from Sonomura did
not reach me until early September.

"Well, look at what we have here! The good doctor has suc-
cumbed at last!"

I felt a surge of affection for Sonomura as I eagerly tore open his
letter. But the very first line caused my face to go pale.

"Please consider this letter my last will and testament ..." Such were the first words of the letter.

Please consider this letter my last will and testament. I anticipate that I will be killed for Eiko's enjoyment tonight. I believe the two of them are planning to take my life using the same method that you and I witnessed before ... This is a fate that I cannot escape; nor do I have any particular desire to escape it. I am about to die, and I want you to know it.

No doubt, this will come as a surprise to you. I can see the pained smile of pity and regret coming to your lips at the thought of my absurd eccentricity and capriciousness. I ask only that you not hate me—and if indeed you do hate me, I beg of you to reconsider. You must understand that the eccentricity that led me to throw away my own life is no ordinary eccentricity. I was rude to you the other day. Given my behavior, you had every right to put an end to our friendship. To be perfectly honest, I was so in love with my dear, dear Eiko at the time that I thought nothing of losing my last and only friend for her sake. Indeed I wanted no more of your unsolicited advice and made sure, therefore, to anger you so that you would leave me in peace. I had no concern for my own life—how could I possibly care about our friendship? All of this was the result of my insane love, so please try not to hold it against me. You know me very well. I have no doubt that you will by now have found a way to forgive me for all of that. And tonight, when I take my leave of this life, I am confident that you, with your great understanding and compassion, will find it in your heart to feel pity, and not hatred, for your old friend. I intend to die peacefully with this knowledge.

I do, however, feel obliged to unburden you of any unnecessary worries by offering you a full report of how this affair has come this far and why it is that I have to die. With this letter, then, I both discharge that obligation, and ask you, my dearest friend, to see to a few matters after I am dead.

I could not possibly describe in writing every aspect of how events have unfolded since I last saw you. I will thus record the bare outlines here and leave the rest to your imagination ... To put it simply, the primary reason they are going to kill me is that as of today my existence has become a nuisance to Eiko and has ceased to provide her with any pleasure or profit. She has already relieved me of my entire fortune. I realize now that the only reason she became intimate with me in the first place was because she had her eyes on my family's money ...

I knew this to be true. But I could not help loving her anyway. The second reason has to do with the fact that I gradually came to know their secrets. This, it seems, is the most powerful motivating factor in their plans to kill me. For reasons of self-preservation, they simply cannot allow me to live any longer.

As to how I figured out that they plan to kill me, I will refrain from detailed explanations here and simply refer you to the enclosed letter written in the cryptographic code we discussed before. All will be revealed to you upon reading it. I found it last night, lying on the ground in the garden of my house, so there is no doubt that it is a secret communication between Eiko and the man with the crewcut. They are using the code to discuss their plans to murder me in secret. If you apply the same method of decoding that I described to you the other day, you will see what they have in store for me. To summarize, they plan to use that same method, at that same place, to murder me, tonight, at 12:50 a.m. Upon being strangled by Eiko, I will have my photograph taken like the others. I will then be submerged in the chemical bath. And by tomorrow morning my body will have dissolved into nothing and vanished from the face of the earth. This strikes me as an infinitely better way to die than succumbing to a stroke or being blown to bits by cannon fire. All the more so, since the hand that does it will belong to the woman to whom I have willingly handed over my own life, I can say, without the slightest exaggeration, that I can think of no greater happiness than to end my life in this way.

But it is not yet clear how Eiko plans to lure me all the way to the area behind Suitengū shrine. She and I have plans to attend the Imperial Theater this evening; no doubt she has some scheme to deceive me and lure me there on the way home. I sense some plan like this afoot.

At first my eccentricity compelled me only to be near her. But now I find myself consumed with the desire to sacrifice everything to her. If I cared about my life, there are of course any number of ways in which I could avoid dying tonight. But I do not even dream of surviving. And even if I did, now that I have incurred their hatred, I know that while I might escape their clutches tonight, they will eventually catch up with me. And in any case, I have long desired what this night has in store for me.

But let me reassure you of a few things. While they do seem aware that I have sniffed out some of their secrets, they are not aware that you and I were watching them through the knotholes that night, or that I picked up the secret notes they wrote to each other in code. They have no notion that you exist or that anyone beside myself is privy to their secrets. For this reason, after my death, as long as you choose not to embark on any plan to expose their misdeeds, you will have no reason to fear for your safety. As for the slips of a paper covered in cryptographs that I have enclosed in this letter, I ask that you keep them safe as mementoes of me. But I must implore you never to yield to the temptation to use them as evidence in any plan to convict them for their crimes. That would be rash and ill-advised. I will, of course, also have the consideration for your sake not to utter a word about the knotholes. I want Eiko to believe completely that I died because I was bewitched by her charms and stepped into the trap that she laid. As someone who loves and worships her, this is all the more kind and faithful a thing to do.

From you, I ask only this: will you return to that alleyway in Suitengū, station yourself once again before that knothole, and look on as I breathe my last? Will you watch from the shadows as this person you see before you vanishes from the world? As I explained earlier, Eiko has already taken everything from me. I have not a single penny to bequeath, and no heirs to bequeath it to. Unlike you, I have no literary works to leave as a legacy. Once the chemical bath does its work, my very corpse will dissolve and with it, all traces of my existence will disappear, leaving neither shadow nor shape behind. The fact that I once existed will remain only as a memory in your head. It saddens me to think of this. But at the very least, I want to leave the strongest possible impression of myself on your brain while I am still alive. And I can think of no better way to accomplish this than to have you witness the scene of my death. Knowing that you are looking through the knothole will put my mind at ease and allow me to die without regrets. I know I have taxed your patience enough with my actions thus far, and this further demand no doubt seems the height of selfishness. But I implore you to acquiesce to the fate that has brought us together, and to grant my request.

I wanted to meet with you once more before I died, but those two have stuck very close to me and it was not easy even to find time away from them to write this letter. My only concern at this moment is whether this letter will reach you in time, so that you can be ready by 12:50 a.m. tonight.

I do have one additional, crucial request: you must resist the temptation to give in to your own kindness and attempt to save my life. My desire to die at her hands, I assure you, is not a case of sour grapes. Gratuitous interference on your part, however motivated by feelings of friendship, will only cause me to resent you. It will be the end of our relations. I see no point in maintaining a friendship with someone who is incapable of appreciating my nature.

Sonomura's letter cut off rather abruptly here. It arrived at my house just in time, in the early evening of the day in question.

So what action did I take that evening? Did I reject his earnest plea and report the criminals to the police in an effort to save his life? Or did I grant his request and do my duty as his one and only friend? ... Naturally, I saw no alternative but to choose the latter.

I lack the courage to narrate in detail the scene I witnessed through the knothole that evening. The murder played out in the same way, with one difference: on the previous occasion I had no connection to the man in tails, but now it was my close friend whose gruesome death I saw as plain as day. How indeed, could I muster the presence of mind to describe such a scene?

Having previously followed Sonomura through the dark and labyrinthine alleyways without paying much attention myself, I had forgotten the exact location of the house, and wandered for nearly an hour through the streets before I found it. When I finally did manage to locate the house, there were only five or six minutes remaining before 12:50 ... Needless to say, the fish-scale mark was affixed to the front gate that evening as well. Without it, I would never have been able to recognize the house—but I did find it, and I was able to witness the whole process, from the instant she strangled him, to the taking of the photograph, and finally the moment when the body was hauled into the tub. What's more, while on that earlier evening we had watched the whole scene from behind, on this night the perpetrators and the victim were facing toward the knothole, as if they were performing the scene expressly for my delectation. Even after he died, Sonomura's eyes glared through the knothole, straight into mine. I heard the excruciating, heartrending groans as he flailed in desperation with the silk waistband wrapped tightly around his neck, as she squeezed the last breath out of his body. Then the cold, thin smile that lit up Eiko's face ... and the look of cruel scorn in the eyeballs of the man with the crewcut. I leave it to the reader to imagine how profoundly frightening these images were.

The photographing of the corpse, the preparation of the chemical bath, and all other components of the scene were carried out in the same order, and in the same fashion as before. At the end, when his lifeless body had been submerged in the Western-style tub, Eiko remarked, "This one is thin like Matsumura-san, so it won't take long to dissolve."

"Yes, but he's a lucky one, isn't he? He got his heart's desire: killed by the hand of the woman he loved."

The man said this in a low voice, with a sneering laugh.

I waited for the light to go out, crept back out of the alleyway, and walked in a daze through Ningyō-chō and on to Bakuro-chō.

"So this is the end. The man called Sonomura is no more."

As my thoughts ran on in this way, I felt less sad than disappointed at how quickly it had all taken place. He was always an impetuous and twisted fellow, and now even in death he was perverse. And yet there was something magnificent, I thought, about depravity elevated to this level.

It was in the morning two days later that an envelope containing a single photograph was delivered by post to my address. Upon opening it, I saw that it was indeed the photograph taken two nights earlier of Sonomura's dead body; there was of course no return address.

I turned the photograph over and found this long message written in a hand I did not recognize:

We have heard that Sonomura was a close friend of yours. We have taken the liberty of sending you this photograph as a memento of him. You may have had some news of his mysterious disappearance. The tragic image in this photograph will be enough to fill in the rest of the mystery. In any case, Mr. Sonomura met a violent death on a certain day in a certain month in a certain location.

We have been entrusted with a message for you from Mr. Sonomura. You will find a certain amount of cash in the desk drawer in his study at his home near Shiba Park. This cash is yours to spend as you see fit. He communicated this message to us at the moment he realized the inescapability of his fate, and we hereby bequeath it faithfully to you.

We trust that you are a man of great character and integrity. As long as you do not betray our trust, we have no intention of causing you any trouble.

As soon as I read this line, I locked the photograph up tight in my safe and headed straight for Sonomura's house in Shiba.

And whom should I find there but the man with the crewcut, playing the role of houseboy today just as he had before. I didn't say a word, and he ushered me excitedly into the study in the back of the house.

There, seated in an easy chair in the middle of the room, puffing leisurely on a cigarette, was the very Sonomura who was supposed to have been murdered two days previously.

Something snapped inside me.

"Sonomura, you bastard! You've taken me for a quite a long ride, haven't you?"

As the truth began to dawn on me, I strode to his side.

"What is the meaning of this my friend? Has it all been a tissue of lies? I have worried so much, in my ignorance of your manipulations."

As I said these words I stared intently into his eyes, as if to bore a hole in his face. And yet, while it would have been different if it were anyone else, with Sonomura I could summon no anger.

"I am so sorry, my friend ..."

As he said this, Sonomura stared off into the distance and opened his mouth slowly to speak. His expression wore its customary melancholy look and showed no hint of gloating or satisfaction at having fooled me.

"You were indeed taken for a ride, my dear Takahashi. But I was not the one doing the driving the whole time. In the first half, it was Eiko who was taking me for a ride, and in the second it was I who duped you. But please know that I did not do what I did for the sake of a moment's amusement."

This is how he explained his motive: The woman called Eiko was a former actress in a certain theater troupe, where she had some success thanks to her looks and her intelligence. But on top of being born with corrupt morals, her sexual desires gave her a taste for brutality. These proclivities soon got her expelled from the theater troop, after which she took up with a band of delinquent youths, and with their help she had made a habit of extorting money from wealthy men. Meanwhile, a man named "S," who had previously served as a houseboy for Sonomura, wound up in some trouble, and as a result he became acquainted with Eiko, whom he told all about Sonomura. Here was an eccentric type, "S" told her, with money and too much time on his hands, who spent his days in the pursuit of strange women; he could be difficult, but he was also not entirely of sound mind and might easily be convinced to give up his entire fortune, or even his life, for a woman he was passionate about. With brains and looks like hers, "S" said, Sonomura would be an easy target. "S" promised to formulate a plan that would put Sonomura in her power with a single glance, and he proposed that she give it a try.

So the whole chain of events, from the incident in the cinema where Sonomura retrieved the scrap of paper with the secret code written on it, to the murder of the man in tails in the longhouse in Suitengū, was orchestrated with the help of her male associates, all with the goal of luring Sonomura's eye to that knothole. "S" thought of the bit with the cryptographic alphabet half as a joke. It was the job of the man with the crewcut to make sure that Sonomura picked the note up off the floor. The purple and green chemicals used to dissolve human bodies were of course a total fabrication, and the man in tails was merely pretending to be dead. The story about "Matsumura-san" was cleverly planted to make use of an item she had seen in the paper about the disappearance of the Viscount Matsumura. "S" thus used all of his knowledge of Sonomura's tastes and tendencies to devise a plan that left him utterly bewitched by Eiko.

If this was how Sonomura was tricked by Eiko, the following is how I was tricked by Sonomura. Sonomura realized not soon after he became close to Eiko that he was being manipulated by her; but he could only marvel and rejoice in the extent of the eccentricity of this woman so determined to make a fool out of him—it was an eccentricity that rivaled his own. Indeed, it made him all the more obsessed with her. Even once he knew he had been taken for a ride, he found it impossible to admit that the scene he had witnessed in the alley through the knothole was a lie. He wanted to lose his own life to Eiko, like the man in tails. This desire overtook him like an uncontrollable flood.

He became a mere plaything in Eiko's hands. He gave her all the money and presents she asked for. In the end he had said to her, "My entire fortune is yours if you will use your own hands to kill me like you did before. But this time for real. This is my only request."

Now Eiko may have been a delinquent, but this was one request she could not grant.

"If you can't do it for real, then at least pretend to. I want to arrange for my friend to witness it."

This was Sonomura's request.... As I think about it now it is seems clear that he was motivated not just by idle curiosity but by some peculiar, abnormal sexual drive ...

"Now that I have told you all of this, I hope you'll understand. I did not set out to deceive you. I wanted to believe as much as you did that the man called Sonomura had been murdered by her. I believed that your presence there looking through the knothole would make the mood and the scene of that evening seem all the more real. If only Eiko would allow it, I would happily die for you at any moment."

This was Sonomura's explanation.

Before long, I heard the sound of a light pair of slippers, and Eiko came into the room. She was twirling in both hands the scrap of silk crepe that had played such a frightful role in her mischief. She stood there between the two men, waiting to be introduced to me, undaunted, and smiling.

Afterword

"DEVILS IN DAYLIGHT" IS ONLY A ROUGH APPROXimation of the original title of this novella, which, in Japanese, consists of four Chinese characters: 白昼鬼語, pronounced *haku-chūki-go*. The phrase has the air of some venerable expression from the Chinese classics, many of which likewise consist of four characters, sententiously crammed together.

On closer inspection, however, the title reveals itself as Tanizaki's fabrication, a punning portmanteau made up of evocative fragments of other phrases. The first two characters (*haku-chū*) suggest the Japanese word for "daydream" (*haku-chū-mu*), which one dictionary defines as "the viewing of imaginary fantasies as if they were images seen in the light of day." These same two characters are also found in various other Japanese expressions referring to audacious acts carried out "in broad daylight." The second half of the title, *ki-go* means "devils talking." The dictionary lists an obscure definition referring to the voices of nature spirits, such as the sound of the wind or the snow. But it also suggests a homophonous phrase using a different character for "*ki*" (綺語), that means "idle talk" or "deceptive rhetoric." This other *kigo* is one of the "ten evil deeds" in Buddhist doctrine, and an old derogatory term for fiction. Like *Devils* itself then, this made-up title encapsulates many of the themes that preoccupied Tanizaki throughout his career: the play of light and shadow, the pull of fantasy, and the demonic power of fictional narration to create other worlds out of whole cloth. That the title is a "fake" of sorts is a good reminder not to take the text too seriously, but also to tread carefully: Tanizaki's sense of humor may border on camp, but he is dead serious about fiction.

Of course the devils in this story do not operate in daylight. Eiko and the man with the crewcut work in a closed room under the blazing artificial light of an electric bulb. Cinema was barely two decades old in 1918 when *Devils* first appeared in print, and Tanizaki was fascinated with the new art form. Two years later, in 1920, he would suspend his career as novelist to take up a position as a literary consultant for the Taikatsu film studio, collaborating with the director Thomas Kurihara for over two years. In *Devils,* he appears to be using writing to explore the potential of film. In the first scene at the house with the fish-scale mark, Sonomura and Takahashi look through their respective knotholes as if peering through the viewfinder of a movie camera. The restricted perspective heightens the suspense as bodies move in and out of the frame; then we zoom in for a "close-up" from behind of the nape of Eiko's neck. In the earlier scene where Sonomura first happens upon the mysterious threesome, the setting is an actual cinema showing "moving pictures." And yet no one is interested in what is happening on the screen in front of them. The drama is behind the seats, on scraps of paper written in a secret code derived from a work of literature: Edgar Allan Poe's 1848 story "The Gold Bug." In his essay "The Present and Future of Moving Pictures," written in 1917, the year before *Devils,* Tanizaki noted that Poe's works would be particularly well suited to film adaptations.* *Devils in Daylight* is perhaps Tanizaki's way of exploring what that might look like, using only words on the page.

But *Devils* is about much more than the relation between cinema and literature. It is a tale of the rivalry between literature and a number of other media forms. The murder scene that plays out in front of Sonomura and Takahashi's eyes combines elements of cinema, literature, photography, and live theater. But this being Tanizaki, the point is less to see which one wins than to enjoy the effects produced by multiple layers of mediation. Why stay at home writing a novel, Sonomura asks Takahashi, when you have a chance to watch an actual murder being committed in the flesh? But wait! Hasn't the question itself come to us in the pages of a work of fiction?

"The Gold Bug" was the most popular of Poe's stories when he was alive. It remains etched in the American consciousness to such a degree that the poet and critic Daniel Hoffman once doubted there was anyone left who hadn't read it.** Poe was also wildly popular in Japan beginning in the 1890s, when Lafcadio Hearn lectured about his works to the elite students at Tokyo Imperial University. Tanizaki often drew on Poe in his early work, and by the early twentieth century, he could rely on a Japanese readership for whom the American writer was already part of the local landscape: "The Gold Bug" had been translated into Japanese and published in a volume together with the English original in 1902. Later it would be retranslated by Tanizaki's brother Tanizaki Seiji, a professor of American literature at Waseda University in Tokyo,

---

* This essay, along with several other pieces of Tanizaki's film-related criticism and fiction, have been translated, with accompanying essays, in Thomas Lamarre, *Shadows on the Screen: Tanizaki Jun'ichirō on Cinema.*

** Daniel Hoffman, *Poe, Poe, Poe, Poe, Poe, Poe, Poe.*

who was among the most prolific translators of Poe into Japanese in the prewar period.*

Of course *Devils in Daylight* is itself a kind of translation of "The Gold Bug." Tanizaki takes the bare outlines of his plot and the narrative frame from Poe, and changes the setting from swampy Sullivan's island off the North Carolina coast to the streets of Taishō-period Tokyo. Poe's tale is told from the perspective of a narrator whose friend "William Legrand" is a lot like Tanizaki's Sonomura—brilliant but "disposed to lunacy." Legrand has discovered a map with clues written in a secret code. He cracks the code using a method that he takes great pleasure in describing to the narrator, and the map leads the two of them, together with Legrand's manumitted slave Jupiter, to Captain Kidd's buried treasure. The discovery makes them all fabulously rich—but the story involves more than wish fulfillment. It ends with the discovery of skeletons underneath the treasure chest, alluding to the murder of Kidd's helpers when the treasure was first buried, as well as the untold violence that went into acquiring it. In Tanizaki's *Devils*, Captain Kidd's treasure morphs from a chest of gold to the scene of a murder, and the riches to be enjoyed are more perverse than pecuniary. If Poe's story ends with real murders in the past, Tanizaki's begins with a faked murder in the future. While the skeletons in "The Gold Bug" make Poe's characters and his readers complicit in piratic violence, casting a dark cloud over the story's celebration of scientific rationality and code-cracking detective work, *Devils* pronounces its own ironic verdict on the voyeurism that beats at the heart of the detective novel genre.

Tanizaki had a good command of English and most scholars

---

* For the history of the reception of Poe in Japan and an extensive bibliography, see Miyanaga Takashi, *Pō to Nihon: sono juyō no rekishi*.

agree that he would have read Poe's "The Gold Bug" both in English and in Japanese translation. For this reason, it seemed appropriate to put some of Poe's own language back into the translation by lifting phrases directly from "The Gold Bug" where Tanizaki seemed to be doing the same. Lovers of Poe will recognize the phrases "stricken with lunacy" and "aberrant of mind" in this translation. Readers themselves will judge if I have gone too far with this strategy. (For the record, I did resist calling those slips of paper bearing cryptographic messages "parchment," or "foolscap"!)

In one case, I borrowed Poe's language to accord with the spirit, rather than the letter, of Tanizaki's adaptation. In the first sentence of "The Gold Bug," the narrator introduces his eccentric friend: "Many years ago, I contracted an intimacy with a Mr. William Legrand." Tanizaki echoes this setup in the opening of *Devils in Daylight*, where Takahashi introduces his friend Sonomura, but does not attempt a direct translation of the remarkable phrase, "contracted an intimacy." In the Japanese text, Takahashi simply "associates" with Sonomura, but I took the liberty of rendering it as "contracted an intimacy" so as to create a stronger echo of Poe's story at the outset. I want to think Tanizaki would have approved. He clearly caught the layers of meaning in this extraordinary phrase. He took the paradox inherent in the idea of a contractual negotiation of intimacy and infused it into his depiction of the close but wary relationship between Takahashi and Sonomura. Takahashi also "contracts" his friendship with Sonomura as if it were a disease, an association born out a few lines later when he worries about Sonomura's madness infecting him over the telephone. And finally, the phrase calls to mind the intimate and fundamentally masochistic contract that readers enter into with authors when they willingly surrender themselves to whatever daytime visions the author cares to dream up.

94

Most accounts of Tanizaki portray him as drawing inspiration at this early stage of his career chiefly from Western writers such as Poe. But in *Devils,* he is equally engaged with the Japanese tradition, especially Lady Murasaki's great eleventh-century novel *The Tale of Genji.* One of many Genji-like moments in *Devils* comes in the scene where Takahashi and Sonomura first glimpse Eiko. Those knotholes are not only like movie cameras, they also recall the classical trope of "peeking through the blinds," (*kaimami*) as Prince Genji does when he first spies the young Murasaki, who will become his great love. When Takahashi expresses his satisfaction at having discovered a woman as beautiful as Eiko in such an "unexpected place," readers of Genji will be reminded of the moment when Genji comes upon the "Lady of the Evening Faces" in her ramshackle, vine-covered house.*

But more than any single theme or trope, what Tanizaki took from Lady Murasaki was her belief in the value of fiction itself. In the Japanese middle ages, devout Buddhists regularly condemned Murasaki to hell for the sin of writing fiction. When they did so, they called fiction "idle talk," or *kigo*: that homophone of the second word in Tanizaki's title, and one of the "ten evil deeds." In Tanizaki's day, the Japanese literary establishment was similarly

---

* Genji's meeting with Yūgao is foretold in the "rainy night discussion" in the "Broom Cypress" chapter, when Genji and his friends discuss the various types of women that attract them. The Fujiwara Warden's comments sound like a summary of *Devils,* except of course that Tanizaki turns the "defenseless girl" into a formidable *femme fatale*: "Beyond these types, you sometimes unexpectedly come across an adorable, defenseless girl whose existence is unknown to court society. She lives in a lonely, sublimely dilapidated residence shut away from the world behind a gate overgrown with weeds and so of course you think of her as an exceptionally rare find. You're mysteriously drawn to her, your imagination stimulated by the things that make her different, and you wonder how she could have ended up in a place like this." (The translation is by Dennis Washburn.)

dismissive of fiction and obsessed with confessional truthfulness and sincerity, even in novels. But Tanizaki was among the proud and self-conscious inheritors of a tradition that may be unique in the world in having the *Tale of Genji*—a piece of "idle talk," written by a woman—occupy the very apex of its classical canon. When Takahashi accepts Sonomura's invitation to watch a murder happen without intervening to stop it, little does this writer know that he is about to witness a work of fiction authored by a woman. Clearly, he has given too much credence to "devils speaking in broad daylight." And yet something about the scenario is evocative—for some, no doubt, uncomfortably so—of the vicarious core of all detective fiction, and perhaps, indeed, of all fictional experiences. As one of the great *Genji* scholars of the nineteenth century put it, and as Tanizaki himself knew well, "all made-up tales are by definition things that are created," and thus full of "apparitions which take astonishing forms."*

Devils in Daylight was serialized simultaneously in the Osaka and Tokyo editions of the *Mainichi shinbun* from May 23 to July 11, 1918. Junichiro Tanizaki was born in Tokyo in 1886. His writing career spanned more than five decades, beginning with his 1911 short story "The Tattooer," about a man who drugs a beautiful woman and tattoos an enormous spider on her back, only to fall hopelessly under her spell when she awakens. He died in 1965, at his home in Yugawara, southwest of Tokyo.

J. KEITH VINCENT

---

* The scholar is Hagiwara Hiromichi (1815–1863), as quoted in Noguchi Takehiko, "Flowers with a Very Human Name: One *Kokugaku* Scholar Pursues the Truth about the Mysterious Death of Yūgao."